A landmark event—an

RAY BR

FROM THE DUST
RETURNED

They have lived for centuries in a house of legend and mystery in upper Illinois—and they are *not* like other Midwesterners. Rarely encountered in daylight hours, some of them have survived since before the Sphinx first sank its paws deep in Egyptian sands. And some sleep in beds with lids.

Now the House is being readied for the gala home-coming that will gather together the far-flung branches of this odd and remarkable clan. But in the midst of eager anticipation, a sense of doom pervades. For the world is changing. And death, no stranger, will always shadow this most singular family . . .

"Filled with poetic imagery, paeans to yesterday and lost faith, and plenty of magic storytelling, *From the Dust Returned* is ample proof that Bradbury hasn't lost the passion and the fire of his youth."
St. Louis Post-Dispatch

(please turn the page for more resounding praise)

"*From the Dust Returned* is as much poetry as fiction.
Images abound, lyrical, heartbreaking."
Baltimore Sun

"A novel funny, beautiful, sad, and wise, to rank with
his finest work. Full of wide-eyed wonder and dazzling
imagery, the stories retain as an integrated whole their
original freshness and charm. . . . This book will shame
the cynics and delight the true believers who never
lost faith in their beloved author."
Publishers Weekly (*Starred Review*)

"One of the greats of twentieth century American
fantasy . . . *From the Dust Returned* revisits dreams
begun when our land had other preoccupations—
ones that seemed grave enough at the time, but now
seem reassuringly manageable. . . . The message is
certainly timely. . . . It warns of witch hunts, a danger
again as it was in the McCarthy era. . . . Not everyone
who looks scary is dangerous; not everyone who
looks normal means well."
Newsday

"Written in trademark Bradbury style, the book reads
like liquid poetry while telling the interconnected
stories of a number of unusual—yet strangely
familiar—family members. . . . A new novel
by Bradbury is an event worth noting."
Library Journal (*Starred Review*)

(more on the following pages)

Books by Ray Bradbury

Bradbury Speaks
The Cat's Pajamas • *Bradbury Stories*
Dandelion Wine • *Dark Carnival*
Death Is a Lonely Business • *Driving Blind*
Fahrenheit 451 • *The Farewell Summer*
From the Dust Returned • *The Golden Apples of the Sun*
A Graveyard for Lunatics • *Green Shadows, White Whale*
The Halloween Tree • *I Sing the Body Electric!*
The Illustrated Man • *Journey to Far Metaphor*
Kaleidoscope • *Let's All Kill Constance*
Long After Midnight • *The Martian Chronicles*
The Machineries of Joy • *A Medicine for Melancholy*
Now and Forever • *The October Country*
One More for the Road • *One Timeless Spring*
Quicker Than the Eye • *R is for Rocket*
The Stories of Ray Bradbury • *S is for Space*
The Toynbee Convector • *We'll Always Have Paris*
When Elephants Last in the Dooryard Bloomed
Yestermorrow • *Zen in the Art of Writing*

RAY BRADBURY

FROM THE DUST RETURNED

AVON BOOKS
An Imprint of HarperCollins*Publishers*

This is a work of fiction. Names, characters, places, and incidents are products of the author's imagination or are used fictitiously and are not to be construed as real. Any resemblance to actual events, locales, organizations, or persons, living or dead, is entire coincidental.

Page 268 serves as a continuation of this copyright page.

AVON BOOKS
An Imprint of HarperCollins*Publishers*
195 Broadway
New York, NY, 10007

Copyright © 2001 by Ray Bradbury
Excerpts from *Dandelion Wine* copyright © 1946, 1947, 1950, 1951, 1952, 1953, 1954, 1955, 1957, copyright © 1956, 1957 by The Curtis Publishing Company; *The Illustrated Man* copyright © 1951; *The Martian Chronicles* copyright © 1946, 1948, 1949, 1950, 1958; *The October Country* copyright © 1943, 1944, 1945, 1946, 1947, 1954, 1955; *Something Wicked This Way Comes* copyright © 1962, 1997; *Death Is a Lonely Business* copyright © 1999; *A Graveyard for Lunatics* copyright © 1990 by Ray Bradbury
ISBN: 0-380-78961-2
www.avonbooks.com

First Avon Books paperback printing: September 2002
First William Morrow hardcover printing: October 2001

Avon Trademark Reg. U.S. Pat. Off. and in Other Countries, Marca Registrada, Hecho en U.S.A.
HarperCollins ® is a trademark of HarperCollins Publishers Inc.

Printed in the U.S.A.

HB 05.11.2023

CONTENTS

CONTENTS

CONTENTS

xiii

CONTENTS

CONTENTS

The Beautiful One Is Here

In the attic where the rain touched the roof softly on spring days and where you could feel the mantle of snow outside, a few inches away, on December nights, A Thousand Times Great Grandmère existed. She did not live, nor was she eternally dead, she . . . existed.

And now with the Great Event about to happen, the Great Night arriving, the Homecoming about to explode, she must be visited!

"Ready? Here I come!" Timothy's voice cried faintly beneath a trapdoor that trembled. "Yes!?"

Silence. The Egyptian mummy did not twitch.

She stood propped in a dark corner like an ancient

dried plum tree, or an abandoned and scorched ironing board, her hands and wrists trussed across her dry riverbed bosom, a captive of time, her eyes slits of deep blue lapis lazuli behind thread-sewn lids, a glitter of remembrance as her mouth, with a shriveled tongue wormed in it, whistled and sighed and whispered to recall every hour of every lost night four thousand years back when she was a pharaoh's daughter dressed in spider linens and warm-breath silks with jewels burning her wrists as she ran in the marble gardens to watch the pyramids erupt in the fiery Egyptian air.

Now Timothy lifted the trapdoor lid of dust to call into that midnight attic world.

"Oh, Beautiful One!"

A faint pollen of dust fell from the ancient mummy's lips.

"Beautiful no longer!"

"Grandma, then."

"Not Grandma merely," came the soft response.

"A Thousand Times *Great* Grandmère?"

"Better." The old voice dusted the silent air. "Wine?"

"Wine." Timothy rose, a small flacon in his hands.

"The vintage, child?" the voice murmured.

"B.C., Grandmère."

"How many years?"

"Two thousand, almost *three*, B.C."

"Excellent." Dust fell from the withered smile. "Come."

Picking his way through a litter of papyrus, Timothy reached the no-longer Beautiful One, whose voice was still incredibly lovely.

"Child?" said the withered smile. "Do you fear me?"

"*Always,* Grandmère."

"Wet my lips, child."

He reached to let the merest drop wet the lips that now trembled.

"More," she whispered.

Another drop of wine touched the dusty smile.

"*Still* afraid?"

"No, Grandmère."

"Sit."

He perched on the lid of a box with hieroglyphs of warriors and doglike gods and gods with lions' heads painted on it.

"Why are you here?" husked the voice beneath the serene riverbed face.

"Tomorrow's the Great Night, Grandmère, I've waited for all my life! The Family, *our* Family, coming, flying in from all over the world! Tell me, Grandmère, how it all began, how this House was built and where we came from and—"

"Enough!" the voice cried, softly. "Let me recall a

thousand noons. Let me swim down the deep well. Stillness?"

"Stillness."

"Now," came the whisper across four thousand years, "here's how it was . . ."

CHAPTER I

The Town and the Place

At first, A Thousand Times Great Grandmère said, there was only a place on the long plain of grass and a hill on which was nothing at all but more grass and a tree that was as crooked as a fork of black lightning on which nothing grew until the town came and the House arrived.

We all know how a town can gather need by need until suddenly its heart starts up and circulates the people to their destinations. But how, you ask, does a house arrive?

The fact is that the tree was there and a lumberman passing to the Far West leaned against it, and guessed it to be before Jesus sawed wood and shaved planks in his father's yard or Pontius Pilate washed his palms. The

tree, some said, beckoned the House out of tumults of weather and excursions of Time. Once the House was there, with its cellar roots deep in Chinese tombyards, it was of such a magnificence, echoing facades last seen in London, that wagons, intending to cross the river, hesitated with their families gazing up and decided if this empty place was good enough for a papal palace, a royal monument, or a queen's abode, there hardly seemed a reason to leave. So the wagons stopped, the horses were watered, and when the families looked, they found their shoes as well as their souls had sprouted roots. So stunned were they by the House up there by the lightning-shaped tree, that they feared if they left the House would follow in their dreams and spoil all the waiting places ahead.

So the House arrived first and its arrival was the stuff of further legends, myths, or drunken nonsense.

It seems there was a wind that rose over the plains bringing with it a gentle rain that turned into a storm that funneled a hurricane of great strength. Between midnight and dawn, this portmanteau-storm lifted any moveable object between the fort towns of Indiana and Ohio, stripped the forests in upper Illinois, and arrived over the as-yet-unborn site, settled, and with the level hand of an unseen god deposited, shakeboard by shakeboard and shingle by shingle, an arousal of timber that shaped itself long before sunrise as something dreamed of by Rameses but finished by Napoleon fled from dreaming Egypt.

There were enough beams within to roof St. Peter's and enough windows to sun-blind a bird migration. There was a porch skirted all around with enough space to rock a celebration of relatives and boarders. Inside the windows loomed a cluster, a hive, a maze of rooms, sufficient to a roster, a squad, a battalion of as yet unborn legions, but haunted by the promise of their coming.

The House, then, was finished and capped before the stars dissolved into light and it stood alone on its promontory for many years, somehow failing to summon its future children. There must be a mouse in every warren, a cricket on every hearth, smoke in the multitudinous chimneys, and creatures, almost human, icing every bed. Then: mad dogs in yards, live gargoyles on roofs. All waited for some immense thunderclap of the long departed storm to shout: *Begin!*

And, finally, many long years later, it did.

CHAPTER 2

Anuba Arrives

The cat came first, in order to be *absolute* first.

It arrived when all the cribs and closets and cellar bins and attic hang-spaces still needed October wings, autumn breathings, and fiery eyes. When every chandelier was a lodge and every shoe a compartment, when every bed ached to be occupied by strange snows and every banister anticipated the down-slide of creatures more pollen than substance, when every window, warped with ages, distorted faces looking from shadows, when every empty chair seemed occupied by things unseen, when every carpet desired invisible footfalls and the water pump on the back stoop inhaled, sucking vile liquors toward a surface

abandoned because of the possible upchuck of night-mares, when all the parquetry planks whined with the oil-ings of lost souls, and when all the weathercocks on the high roofs gyred in the wind and smiled griffin teeth, while deathwatch beetles ticked behind the walls . . .

Only then did the royal cat named Anuba arrive.

The front door slammed.

And there was Anuba.

Clothed in a fine pelt of arrogance, her quiet engine quieter, centuries before limousines. She paced the corri-dors, a noble creature just come from a journey of three thousand years.

It had commenced with Rameses when, shelved and stored at his royal feet, she had slept away some few cen-turies with another shipload of cats, mummified and linen-wrapped, to be awakened when Napoleon's assas-sins had tried to gun-pock the lion icon Sphinx's face be-fore the Mamelukes' gunpowder shot them into the sea. Whereupon the cats, with this queen feline, had loitered in shop alleys until Victoria's locomotives crossed Egypt, using tomb-filchings and the asphalt linen-wrapped dead for fuel. These packets of bones and flammable tar churned the stacks in what was called the Nefertiti-Tut Express. The black smokes firing the Egyptian air were haunted by Cleopatra's cousins who blew off, flaking the wind until the Express reached Alexandria, where the still unburned cats and their Empress Queen shipped out for the States, bundled in great spools of papyrus bound for a paper-mashing plant in Boston where, unwound, the cats fled as cargo on wagon trains while the papyrus, unleafed among innocent stationery printers, murdered two or three hundred profiteers with terrible miasmal bacteria. The hospitals of New England were chock-full of Egyptian maladies that soon brimmed the graveyards, while the cats, cast off in Memphis, Tennessee, or Cairo, Illinois, walked the rest of the way to the town of the dark tree, the high and most peculiar House.

And so Anuba, her fur a sooty fire, her whiskers like lightning sparks, with ocelot paws strolled into the House on that special night, ignoring the empty rooms and dreamless beds, to arrive at the main hearth in the great parlor. Even as she turned thrice to sit, a fire exploded in the cavernous fireplace.

While upstairs, fires on a dozen hearths inflamed themselves as this queen of cats rested.

The smokes that churned up the chimneys that night recalled the sounds and spectral sights of the Nefertiti-Tut Express thundering the Egyptian sands, scattering mummy linens popped wide as library books, informing the winds as they went.

And that, of course, was only the first arrival.

CHAPTER 3

The High Attic

"And who came second, Grandmère, who came *next*?"

"The Sleeper Who Dreams, child."

"What a fine name, Grandmère. Why did the Sleeper come here?"

"The High Attic called her across the world. The attic above our heads, the second most important high garret that funnels the winds and speaks its voice in the jet streams across the world. The dreamer had wandered those streams in storms, photographed by lightnings, anxious for a nest. And here she came and there she is now! Listen!"

A Thousand Times Great Grandmère slid her lapis lazuli gaze upward.

"Listen."

And above, in a further layer of darkness, some semblance of dream stirred . . .

CHAPTER 4

The Sleeper and Her Dreams

Long before there was anyone to listen, there was the High Attic Place, where the weather came in through broken glass, from wandering clouds going nowhere, somewhere, anywhere, and made the attic talk to itself as it laid out a Japanese sand garden of dust across its planks.

What the breezes and winds whispered and murmured as they shook the poorly laid shingles no one could say except Cecy, who came soon after the cat to become the fairest and most special daughter of the Family as it settled in with her talent for touching other people's ears, thence inward to their minds and still further their dreams; there she stretched herself out on the ancient Japanese garden sands and let the small dunes shift her as the wind played the rooftop. There she heard the languages of weather and far places and knew what went beyond this hill, or the sea on one hand and a farther sea on the other, including the age-old ice which blew from the north and the forever summer that breathed softly from the Gulf and the Amazon wilds.

So, lying asleep, Cecy inhaled the seasons and heard the rumorings of towns on the prairies over the mountains and if you asked her at meals she would tell you the violent or serene occupations of strangers ten thousand miles away. Her mouth was always full of gossips of people being born in Boston or dying in Monterey, heard during the night as her eyes were shut.

The Family often said if you stashed Cecy in a music box like those prickly brass cylinders and turned her, she would play the ships coming in or the ships in departure and, why not, all the geographies of this blue world, and then again, the universe.

She, in sum, was a goddess of wisdom, and the Family, knowing this, treated her like porcelain, let her sleep all hours, knowing that when she woke, her mouth would echo twelve tongues and twenty sets of mind, philosophies enough to crack Plato at noon or Aristotle at midnight.

And the High Attic waited now, with its Arabian seashores of dust, and its Japanese pure white sands, and the shingles shifted and whispered, remembering a future just hours ahead, when the nightmare delights came home.

So the High Attic whispered.

And, listening, Cecy quickened.

Before the tumult of wings, the collision of fogs and mists and souls like ribboned smokes, she saw her own soul and hungers.

Make haste, she thought. Oh, quickly now! Run forth. Fly fast. For what?

"I want to be in love!"

CHAPTER 5

The Wandering Witch

Into the air, over the valleys, under the stars, above a river, a pond, a road, flew Cecy. Invisible as autumn winds, fresh as the breath of clover rising from twilight fields, she flew. She soared in doves as soft as white ermine, stopped in trees and lived in leaves, showering away in fiery hues when the breeze blew. She perched in a lime-green frog, cool as mint by a shining pool. She trotted in a brambly dog and barked to hear echoes from the sides of distant barns. She lived in dandelion ghosts or sweet clear liquids rising from the musky earth.

Farewell summer, thought Cecy. I'll be in every living thing in the world tonight.

Now she inhabited neat crickets on the tar-pool roads, now prickled in dew on an iron gate.

"Love," she said. "Where is my love!?"

She had said it at supper. And her parents had stiffened back in their chairs. "Patience," they advised. "Remember, you're remarkable. Our whole Family is odd and remarkable. We must not marry with ordinary folk. We'd lose our dark souls if we did. You wouldn't want to lose your ability to 'travel' by wish and desire, would you? Then be careful. Careful!"

But in her high attic room, Cecy had touched perfume to her throat and stretched out, trembling and apprehensive, on her four-poster, as a moon the color of milk rose over Illinois country, turning rivers to cream and roads to platinum.

"Yes," she sighed. "I'm one of an odd family that flies nights like black kites. I can live in anything at all—a pebble, a crocus, or a praying mantis. Now!"

The wind whipped her away over fields and meadows.

She saw the warm lights of cottages and farms glowing with twilight colors.

If I can't be in love, myself, she thought, because I'm odd, then I'll be in love through someone else!

Outside a farmhouse in the fresh night a dark-haired girl, no more than nineteen, drew up water from a deep stone well, singing.

Cecy fell—a dry leaf—into the well. She lay in the tender moss of the well, gazing up through dark coolness. Now she quickened in a fluttering, invisible amoeba. Now in a water droplet! At last, within a cold cup, she felt herself lifted to the girl's warm lips. There was a soft night sound of drinking.

Cecy looked out from the girl's eyes.

She entered into the dark head and gazed from the shining eyes at the hands pulling the rough rope. She listened through the shell ears to this girl's world. She smelled a particular universe through these delicate nostrils, felt this special heart beating, beating. Felt this strange tongue move with singing.

The girl gasped. She stared into the night meadows.

"Who's there?"

No answer.

Only the wind, whispered Cecy.

"Only the wind." The girl laughed, but shivered.

It was a good body, this girl's. It held bones of finest slender ivory hidden and roundly fleshed. This brain was like a pink tea rose, hung in darkness, and there was cider wine in this mouth. The lips lay firm on the white, white teeth and the brows arched neatly at the world, and the hair blew soft and fine on her milky neck. The pores knit small and close. The nose tilted at the moon and the cheeks glowed like small fires. The body drifted with feather-balances from one motion to another and seemed always humming to itself. Being in this body was like basking in a hearth fire, living in the purr of a sleeping cat, stirring in warm creek waters that flowed by night to the sea.

Yes! thought Cecy.

"What?" asked the girl, as if she'd heard.

What's your name? asked Cecy carefully.

"Ann Leary." The girl twitched. "Now why should I say that out loud?"

Ann, Ann, whispered Cecy. *Ann, you're going to be in love.*

As if to answer this, a great roar sprang from the road, a clatter and a ring of wheels on gravel. A tall man drove up in an open car, holding the wheel with his monstrous arms, his smile glowing across the yard.

"Ann!"

"Is that you, Tom?"

"Who else?" He leaped from the car, laughing.

"I'm not speaking to you!" Ann whirled, the bucket in her hands slopping.

No! cried Cecy.

Ann froze. She looked at the hills and the first stars. She stared at the man named Tom. Cecy made her drop the bucket.

"Look what you've done!"

Tom ran up.

"Look what you made me do!"

He wiped her shoes with a kerchief, laughing.

"Get away!" She kicked at his hands, but he laughed again, and gazing down on him from miles away, Cecy saw the turn of his head, the size of his skull, the flare of his nose, the shine of his eyes, the girth of his shoulders, and the hard strength of his hands doing this delicate thing with the handkerchief. Peering down from the secret attic of this lovely head, Cecy yanked a hidden copper ventriloquist's wire and the pretty mouth popped wide: "Thank you!"

"Oh, so you have manners?" The smell of leather on his hands, the smell of the open car from his clothes into the tender nostrils, and Cecy, far, far away over night meadows and autumn fields, stirred as with some dream in her bed.

"Not for you, no!" said Ann.

Hush, speak gently, said Cecy. She moved Ann's fingers out toward Tom's head. Ann snatched them back.

"I've gone mad!"

"You have." He nodded, smiling but bewildered. "Were you going to touch me?"

"I don't know. Oh, go away!" Her cheeks glowed with pink charcoals.

"Run! I'm not stopping you." Tom got up. "Changed your mind? Will you go to the dance with me tonight?"

"No," said Ann.

Yes! cried Cecy. *I've never danced. I've never worn a long gown, all rustly. I want to dance all night. I've never known what it's like to be in a woman, dancing; Father and Mother would not permit. Dogs, cats, locusts, leaves, everything else in the world at one time or another I've known, but never a woman in the spring, never on a night like this. Oh, please—we must dance!*

She spread her thought like the fingers of a hand within a new glove.

"Yes," said Ann Leary. "I don't know why, but I'll go with you tonight, Tom."

Now inside, quick! cried Cecy. *Wash, tell your folks, get your gown, into your room!*

"Mother," said Ann, "I've changed my mind!"

The car was roaring down the pike, the rooms of the farmhouse jumped to life, water was churning the bath, the mother was rushing about with a fringe of hairpins in her mouth. "What's come over you, Ann? You don't like Tom!"

"True." Ann stopped amidst the great fever.

27

But it's farewell summer! thought Cecy. *Summer back before the winter comes.*

"Summer," said Ann. "Farewell."

Fine for dancing, thought Cecy.

". . . dancing," murmured Ann Leary.

Then she was in the tub and the soap creaming on her white seal shoulders, small nests of soap beneath her arms, and the flesh of her warm breasts moving in her hands and Cecy moving the mouth, making the smile, keeping the actions going. There must be no pause, or the entire pantomime might fall in ruins! Ann Leary must be kept moving, doing, acting, wash here, soap there, now out!

"You!" Ann caught herself in the mirror, all whiteness and pinkness like lilies and carnations. "Who are—?"

A girl seventeen. Cecy gazed from her violet eyes. *You can't see me. Do you know I'm here?*

Ann Leary shook her head. "I've loaned my body to a last-of-summer witch, for sure."

Close! laughed Cecy. *Now, dress!*

The luxury of feeling fine silk move over an ample body! Then the halloo outside.

"Ann, Tom's back!"

"Tell him, wait." Ann sat down. "I'm not going to that dance."

"What?" cried her mother.

Cecy snapped to attention. It had been a fatal moment of leaving Ann's body for an instant. She had heard the distant sound of the car rushing through moonlit country and thought, I'll find Tom, sit in his head and see what it's like to be in a man of twenty-two on a night like this. And so she had started quickly down the road, but now, like a bird to a cage, flew back to clamor in Ann's head.

"Ann!"

"Tell him to leave!"

"Ann!"

But Ann had the bit in her mouth. "No, no, I hate him!"

I shouldn't have left—even for a moment. Cecy poured her mind into the hands of the young girl, into the heart, into the head, softly, softly. *Stand up,* she thought.

Ann stood.

Put on your coat!

Ann put on her coat.

March!

"No!"

March!

"Ann," said her mother, "get on out there. What's come over you?"

"Nothing, Mother. Good night. We'll be home late."

Ann and Cecy ran together into the vanishing summer night.

A room full of softly dancing pigeons ruffling their quiet, trailing feathers, a room full of peacocks, a room full of rainbow eyes and lights. And in the center of it, around, around, around, danced Ann Leary.

Oh, it is *a fine evening,* said Cecy.

"Oh, it's a fine evening," said Ann.

"You're odd," said Tom.

The music whirled them in dimness, in rivers of song; they floated, they bobbed, they sank, they rose for air, they gasped, they clutched each other as if drowning and whirled on in fans and whispers and sighs to "Beautiful Ohio."

Cecy hummed. Ann's lips parted. The music came out.

Yes, odd, said Cecy.

"You're not the same," said Tom.

"Not tonight."

"You're not the Ann Leary I knew."

No, not at all, at all, whispered Cecy, miles and miles away. "No, not at all," said the moved lips.

"I've the funniest feeling," said Tom. "About you." He danced her and searched her glowing face, watching for something. "Your eyes, I can't figure it."

Do you see me? asked Cecy.

"You're here, Ann, and you're not." Tom turned her carefully, this way and that.

"Yes."

"Why did you come with me?"

"I didn't want to," said Ann.

"Why, then?"

"Something made me."

"What?"

"I don't know." Ann's voice was faintly hysterical.

Now, now, hush, whispered Cecy. *Hush, that's it. Around, around.*

They whispered and rustled and rose and fell away in the dark room, with the music turning them.

"But you *did* come," said Tom.

"I did," said Cecy and Ann.

"Here." And he danced her lightly out an open door and walked her quietly away from the hall and the music and the people.

They climbed in and sat together in his open car.

"Ann," he said, taking her hands, trembling. "Ann." But the way he said her name it was as if it wasn't her name. He kept glancing into her pale face, and now her eyes were open again. "I used to love you, you know that," he said.

31

"I know."

"But you've always been distant and I didn't want to be hurt."

"We're very young," said Ann.

"No, I mean, I'm sorry," said Cecy.

"What *do* you mean?" Tom dropped her hands.

The night was warm and the smell of the earth shimmered up all about them where they sat, and the fresh trees breathed one leaf against another in a shaking and rustling.

"I don't know," said Ann.

"Oh, but *I* know," said Cecy. "You're tall and you're the finest-looking man in all the world. This is a good evening; this is an evening I'll always remember, being with you." She put out the alien cold hand to find his reluctant hand again and bring it back, and warm it and hold it very tight.

"But," said Tom, blinking, "tonight you're here, you're there. One minute one way, the next minute another. I wanted to take you to the dance tonight for old times' sake. I meant nothing by it when I first asked you. And then, when we were standing at the well, I knew something had changed, really changed, about you. There was something new and soft, something . . ." He groped for a word. "I don't know, I can't say. Something about your voice. And I know I'm in love with you again."

"No," said Cecy. "With me, with *me*."

"And I'm afraid of being in love with you," he said. "You'll hurt me."

"I might," said Ann.

No, no, I'd love you with all my heart! thought Cecy. *Ann, say it for me. Say you'd love him!*

Ann said nothing.

Tom moved quietly closer to put his hand on her cheek.

"I've got a job a hundred miles from here. Will you miss me?"

"Yes," said Ann and Cecy.

"May I kiss you goodbye?"

"Yes," said Cecy before anyone else could speak.

He placed his lips to the strange mouth. He kissed the strange mouth and he was trembling.

Ann sat like a white statue.

Ann! said Cecy. *Move!* Hold *him!*

Ann sat like a carved doll in the moonlight.

Again he kissed her lips.

"I do love you," whispered Cecy. "I'm here, it's me you see in her eyes, and I love you if she never will."

He moved away and seemed like a man who had run

a long distance. "I don't know what's happening. For a moment there . . ."

"Yes?"

"For a moment I thought—" He put his hands to his eyes. "Never mind. Shall I take you home now?"

"Please," said Ann Leary.

Tiredly he drove the car away. They rode in the thrum and motion of the moonlit car in the still early, only eleven o'clock summer-autumn night, with the shining meadows and empty fields gliding by.

And Cecy, looking at the fields and meadows, thought, It would be worth it, it would be worth everything to be with him from this night on. And she heard her parents' voices again, faintly, "Be careful. You wouldn't want to be diminished, would you—married to a mere earth-bound creature?"

Yes, yes, thought Cecy, even that I'd give up, here and now, if he would have me. I wouldn't need to roam the lost nights then, I wouldn't need to live in birds and dogs and cats and foxes, I'd need only to be with him. Only him.

The road passed under, whispering.

"Tom," said Ann at last.

"What?" He stared coldly at the road, the trees, the sky, the stars.

"If you're ever, in years to come, at any time, in Green

Town, Illinois, a few miles from here, will you do me a favor?"

"What?"

"Will you do me the favor of stopping and seeing a friend of mine?" Ann Leary said this haltingly, awkwardly.

"Why?"

"She's a good friend. I've told her of you. I'll give you her address." When the car stopped at her farm she drew forth a pencil and paper from her small purse and wrote in the moonlight, pressing the paper to her knee. "Can you read it?"

He glanced at the paper and nodded bewilderedly.

He read the words.

"Will you visit her someday?" Ann's mouth moved.

"Someday."

"Promise?"

"What has this to do with us?" he cried savagely. "What do I want with names and papers?" He crumpled the paper into a tight ball.

"Oh, please promise!" begged Cecy.

". . . promise . . ." said Ann.

"All right, all right, now let be!" he shouted.

I'm tired, thought Cecy. I can't stay. I must go home. I can only travel a few hours each night, moving, flying. But before I go . . .

". . . before I go," said Ann.

She kissed Tom on the lips.

"This is *me* kissing you," said Cecy.

Tom held her off and looked at Ann Leary and looked deep, deep inside. He said nothing, but his face began to relax slowly, very slowly, and the lines vanished away, and his mouth softened from its hardness, and he looked deep again into the moonlit face held here before him.

Then he lifted her out and without so much as good night drove quickly down the road.

Cecy let go.

Ann Leary, crying out, released from prison, it seemed, raced up the moonlit path to her house and slammed the door.

Cecy lingered for only a little while. In the eyes of a cricket she saw the warm night world. In the eyes of a frog she sat for a lonely moment by a pool. In the eyes of a night bird she looked down from a tall, moon-haunted elm and saw the lights go out in two farmhouses, one here, one a mile away. She thought of herself and her Family, and her strange power, and the fact that no one in the Family could ever marry any one of the people in this vast world out here beyond the hills.

Tom? Her weakening mind flew in a night bird under the trees and over deep fields of wild mustard. *Have you still got the paper, Tom? Will you come by someday, some year, sometime, to see me? Will you know me then? Will you look in my face and remember where it was you saw me last and know that you love me as I love you, with all my heart for all time?*

She paused in the cool night air, a million miles from towns and people, above farms and continents and rivers and hills. *Tom?* Softly.

Tom was asleep. It was deep night; his suit was hung on a chair. And in one silent, carefully upflung hand upon the white pillow, by his head, was a small piece of paper with writing on it. Slowly, slowly, a fraction of an inch at a time, his fingers closed down upon and held it tightly. And he did not even stir or notice when a blackbird, faintly, wondrously, beat softly for a moment against the clear moon crystals of the windowpane, then, fluttering quietly, stopped and flew away toward the east, over the sleeping earth.

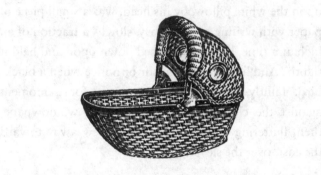

CHAPTER 6

Whence Timothy?

"And *me*, Grandmère?" said Timothy. "Did I come in through the High Attic window?"

"You did not come, child. You were *found*. Left at the door in a basket with Shakespeare for footprop and Poe's *Usher* as pillow. With a note pinned to your blouse: HISTORIAN. You were sent, child, to write us up, list us in lists, register our flights from the sun, our love of the moon. But the House, in a way, *did* call and your small fists hungered to write."

"What, Grandmère, *what*?"

The ancient mouth lisped and murmured and murmured and lisped . . .

"To start with, the House itself . . ."

CHAPTER 7

The House, the Spider, and the Child

The House was a puzzle inside an enigma inside a mystery, for it encompassed silences, each one different, and beds, each a different size, some having lids. Some ceilings were high enough to allow flights with rests where shadows might hang upside down. The dining room nested thirteen chairs, each numbered thirteen so no one would feel left out of the distinctions such numbers implied. The chandeliers above were shaped from the tears of souls in torment at sea five hundred years lost, and the basement cellar kept five hundred vintage-year bins and strange names on the wine tucked therein and empty

cubbies for future visitors who disliked beds or the high ceiling perches.

A network of webways was used by the one and only spider dropping down from above and up from below so the entire House was a sounding spinneret tapestry played on by the ferociously swift Arach, seen one moment by the wine bins and the next in a plummeting rush to the storm-haunted garret, swift and soundless, shuttling the webs, repairing the strands.

How many rooms, cubicles, closets, and bins in all? No one knew. To say one thousand would exaggerate, but one hundred was nowhere near truth. One hundred and fifty nine seems an agreeable amount, and each was empty for a long while, summoning occupants across the world, yearning to pull lodgers from the clouds. The House was a ghost arena, yearning to be haunted. And as the weathers circled Earth for a hundred years, the House became known, and across the world the dead who had lain down for long naps sat up in cold surprise and wished for stranger occupations than being dead, sold off their ghastly trades and prepared for flight.

All of the autumn leaves of the world were shucked and in rustling migrations, hovered mid-America and sifted down to clothe the tree which one moment stood bare and the next was ornamented with autumn falls from the Himalayas, Iceland, and the Capes, in blushed

colors and funeral-somber array, until the tree shook itself to full October flowering and burst forth with fruit
not unlike the cut gourds of All Hallows.

At which time . . .

Someone, passing on the road in dark Dickensian
storms, left a picnic basket by the front iron gate. Within
the basket something wailed and sobbed and cried.

The door opened and a welcoming committee
emerged. This committee consisted of a female, the wife,
extraordinarily tall, and a male, the husband, even taller
and gaunter, and an old woman of an age when Lear
was young, whose kitchen boiled with only kettles and
in the kettles soups better left from menus, and it was
these three who bent to the picnic basket to fold back the
dark cloth over the waiting babe, no more than a week
or two old.

They were astonished at his color, the pink of sunrise
and daybreak, and the sound of his respiration, a spring
bellows, and the beat of his fisting heart, no more than a
hummingbird's caged sound, and on impulse the Lady of
the Fogs and Marshes, for that is how she was known
across the world, held up the smallest of mirrors which
she kept not to study her face, for that was never seen,
but to study the faces of strangers should something be
wrong with them.

"Oh, look," she cried, and held the mirror to the small babe's cheek, and Lo! there was total surprise.

"Curse all and everything," said the gaunt, pale husband. "His face is reflected!"

"He is not like us!"

"No, but *still*," said the wife.

The small blue eyes looked up at them, repeated in the mirror glass. "Leave it," said the husband.

And they might have pulled back and left it to the wild dogs and feral cats, save that at the last instant, the Dark Lady said "No!" and reached to lift, turn, and deliver the basket, babe and all, up the path and into the House and down the hall to a room that became on the instant the nursery, for it was covered on all four walls and topmost ceiling with images of toys put by in Egyptian tombs to nurse the play of pharaohs' sons who traveled a thousand-year river of darkness and had need of joyous instruments to fill dark time and brighten their mouths. So all about on the walls capered dogs, cats; here too were depicted wheatfields to plow through to hide, and loaves of mortality bread and sheaves of green onions for the health of the dead children of some sad pharaoh. And into this tomb nursery came a bright child to stay at the center of a cold kingdom.

And touching the basket, the mistress of the winter-autumn House said, "Was there not a saint with a special light and promise of life called Timothy?"

"Yes."

"So," said the Dark Lady, "lovelier than saints, which stops my doubt and stills my fear, not saint, but Timothy he is. Yes, child?"

And hearing his name, the newcomer in the basket gave a glad cry.

Which rose to the High Attic and caused Cecy in the midst of her dreams to turn in her tidal sleep and lift her head to hear that strange glad cry again which caused her mouth to shape a smile. For while the House stood strangely still, all wondering what might befall them, and as the husband did not move and the wife leaned down half wondering what next to do, Cecy quite instantly knew that her travels were not enough, that beginning now here, now there with seeing and hearing and tasting there must be someone to share it all and tell. And here the teller was, his small cry giving announcement to the fact that no matter what might show and tell, his small hand, grown strong and wild and quick, would capture it and scribble it down. With this assurance sensed, Cecy sent a gossamer of silent thought and welcome to reach the babe and wrap it round and let it know they were as one. And foundling Timothy so touched and comforted gave off his crying and assumed a sleep that was a gift invisible. And seeing this, the frozen husband was given to smile.

And a spider, heretofore unseen, crept from the blanketings, probed all the airs about, then ran to fasten on the small child's hand as nightmare papal ring to bless some future court and all its shadow courtiers, and held so still it seemed but stone of ebony against pink flesh.

And Timothy, all unaware of what his finger wore, knew small refinements of large Cecy's dreams.

CHAPTER 8

Mouse, Far-Traveling

As there was one spider in the House, there had to be—

A singular mouse.

Escaped from life into mortality and a First Dynasty Egyptian tomb, this small ghost rodent at last fled free when some curious Bonaparte soldiers broke the seal and let out great gusts of bacterial air which killed the troops and confused Paris long after Napoleon departed and the Sphinx prevailed, with French gun-pocks in her face, and Fate splayed her paws.

The ghost mouse, so dislodged from darkness, excursioned to a seaport and shipped out with but not among the cats for Marseilles and London and Massachusetts

and a century later, arrived just as the child Timothy cried on the Family's doorstep. This mouse rattle-tapped under the doorsill to be greeted by an alert eight-legged thing, its multiple knees fiddling above its poisonous head. Stunned, Mouse froze in place and wisely did not move for hours. Then, when the arachnid papal ring presence tired of surveillance and departed for breakfast flies, Mouse vanished into the woodwork, rattle-scratched through secret panelings to the nursery. There, Timothy the babe, in need of more fellows no matter how small or strange, welcomed him beneath the blanket to nurse and befriend him for life.

So it was that Timothy, no saint, grew and became a young manchild, with ten candles lit on his anniversary cake.

And the House and the tree and the Family, and Great Grandmère and Cecy in her attic sands, and Timothy with his attendant Arach in one ear and Mouse on his shoulder and Anuba on his lap, waited for the greatest arrival of all . . .

CHAPTER 9

Homecomimg

"Here they come," said Cecy, lying there flat in the High Attic dust.

"Where are they?" cried Timothy near the window, staring out.

"Some of them are over Europe, some over Asia, some of them over the Islands, some over South America!" said Cecy, her eyes closed, the lashes long, brown, and quivering, her mouth opening to let the words whisper out swiftly.

Timothy came forward upon the bare plankings and litters of papyrus. "*Who* are they?"

"Uncle Einar and Uncle Fry, and there's Cousin

William, and I see Frulda and Helgar and Aunt Morgianna, and Cousin Vivian, and I see Uncle Johann! Coming fast!"

"Are they up in the sky?" cried Timothy, his bright eyes flashing. Standing by the bed, he looked no more than his ten years. The wind blew outside; the House was dark and lit only by starlight.

"They're coming through the air and traveling along the ground, in many forms," said Cecy, asleep. She lay motionless and thought inward on herself to tell what she saw. "I see a wolflike thing crossing a dark river—at the shallows—just above a waterfall, the starlight burning his pelt. I see maple leaves blowing high. I see a small bat flying. I see many creature beasts, running under the forest trees and slipping through the highest branches; and they're *all* heading *here*!"

"Will they be here in time?" The spider on Timothy's lapel swung like a black pendulum, excitedly dancing. He leaned over his sister. "In time for the Homecoming?"

"Yes, yes, Timothy!" Cecy stiffened. "Go! Let me travel in the places I love!"

"Thanks!" In the hall, he ran to his room to make his bed. He had awakened at sunset, and as the first stars had risen, he had gone to let his excitement run with Cecy.

The spider hung on a silvery lasso about his slender

neck as he washed his face. "Think, Arach, tomorrow night! All Hallows' Eve!"

He lifted his face to the mirror, the only mirror in the House, his mother's concession to his "illness." Oh, if only he were not so afflicted! He gaped his mouth to show the poor teeth nature had given him. Corn kernels, round, soft, and pale! And his canines? Unsharpened flints!

Twilight was done. He lit a candle, exhausted. This past week the whole small Family had lived as in their old countries, sleeping by day, rousing at sunset to hurry the preparation.

"Oh, Arach, Arach, if only I could *really* sleep days, like all the rest!"

He took up the candle. Oh, to have teeth like steel, like nails! Or the power to send one's mind, free, like Cecy, asleep on her Egyptian sands! But, no, he even feared the dark! He slept in a *bed*! Not in the fine polished boxes below! No wonder the Family skirted him as if he were the bishop's son! If only wings would sprout from his shoulders! He bared his back, stared. No wings. No flight!

Downstairs were slithering sounds of black crepe rising in all the halls, all the ceilings, every door! The scent of burning black tapers rose up the banistered stairwell with Mother's voice and Father's, echoing from the cellar.

"Oh, Arach, will they let me be, really *be,* in the party?" said Timothy. The spider whirled at the end of its silk, alone to itself. "Not just fetch toadstools and cobwebs, hang crepe, or cut pumpkins. But I mean run around, jump, yell, laugh, heck, *be* the party. *Yes!?*"

For answer, Arach spun a web across the mirror, with one word at its center: *Nil!*

All through the House below, the one and only cat ran in a frenzy, the one and only mouse in the echoing wall said the same in nervous graffiti sounds, as if to cry: "The Homecoming!" everywhere.

Timothy climbed back to Cecy, who slept deep. "Where are you now, Cecy?" he whispered. "In the air? On the ground?"

"Soon," Cecy murmured.

"Soon," Timothy beamed. "All Hallows! Soon!"

He backed off studying the shadows of strange birds and loping beasts in her face.

At the open cellar door, he smelled the moist earth air rising. "Father?"

"Here!" Father shouted. "On the double!"

Timothy hesitated long enough to stare at a thousand shadows blowing on the ceilings, promises of arrivals, then he plunged into the cellar.

Father stopped polishing a long box. He gave it a thump. "Shine this up for Uncle Einar!"

Timothy stared.

"Uncle Einar's big! Seven feet?"

"Eight!"

Timothy made the box shine. "And two hundred and sixty pounds?"

Father snorted. "Three hundred! And inside the box?"

"Space for *wings*?" cried Timothy.

"Space," Father laughed, "for wings."

At nine o'clock Timothy leaped out in the October weather. For two hours in the now-warm, now-cold wind he walked the small forest collecting toadstools.

He passed a farm. "If only you knew what's happening at *our* House!" he said to the glowing windows. He climbed a hill and looked at the town, miles away, settling into sleep, the church clock high and round and white in the distance. You don't know, either, he thought.

And carried the toadstools home.

In the cellar ceremony was celebrated, with Father incanting the dark words, Mother's white ivory hands moving in the strange blessings, and all the Family gathered except Cecy, who lay upstairs. But Cecy was there. You saw her peering from now Bion's eyes, now Samuel's, now Mother's, and you felt a movement and now she rolled your eyes and was gone.

Timothy prayed to the darkness.

"Please, please, help me grow to be like them, the ones'll soon be here, who never grow old, can't die, that's what they say, can't die, no matter what, or maybe they died a long time ago but Cecy calls, and Mother and Father call, and Grandmère who only whispers, and now they're coming and I'm nothing, not like them who pass through walls and live in trees or live underneath until seventeen-year rains flood them up and out, and the ones who run in packs, let *me* be one! If they live forever, why not me?"

"Forever," Mother's voice echoed, having heard. "Oh, Timothy, there *must* be a way. Let us *see*! And now—"

The windows rattled. Grandmère's sheath of linen papyrus rustled. Deathwatch beetles in the walls ran amok, ticking.

"Let it begin," Mother cried. "*Begin!*"

And the wind began.

It swarmed the world like a great beast unseen, and the whole world heard it pass in a season of grief and lamentation, a dark celebration of the stuffs it carried to disperse, and all of it funneling upper Illinois. In tidal sweeps and swoons of sound, it robbed the graves of dust from stone angels' eyes, vacuumed the tombs of spectral flesh, seized funeral flowers with no names, shucked druid trees to toss the leaf-harvest high in a dry downpour, a battalion of shorn skins and fiery eyes that burned crazily in oceans of ravening clouds that tore themselves to flags of welcome to pace the occupants of space as they grew in numbers to sound the sky with such melancholy eruptions of lost years that a million farmyard sleepers waked with tears on their faces wondering if it had rained in the night and no one had foretold, and on the storm-river across the sea which roiled at this gravity of leave-taking and arrival until, with a flurry of leaves and dust commingled, it hovered in circles over the hill and the House and the welcoming party and Cecy above all, who in her attic, a slumberous totem on her sands, beckoned with her mind and breathed permission.

Timothy from the highest roof sensed a single blink of Cecy's eyes and—

The windows of the House flew wide, a dozen here, two dozen there, to suck the ancient airs. With every window gaped, all the doors slammed wide, the whole House was one great hungry maw, inhaling night with breaths gasping welcome, welcome, and all of its closets and cellar bins and attic niches shivering in dark tumults!

As Timothy leaned out, a flesh-and-blood gargoyle, the vast armada of tomb dust and web and wing and October leaf and graveyard blossom pelted the roofs even as on the land around the hill shadows trotted the roads and threaded the forests armed with teeth and velvet paws and flickered ears, barking to the moon.

And this confluence of air and land struck the House through every window, chimney, and door. Things that flew fair or in crazed jags, that walked upright or jogged on fours or loped like crippled shades, evicted from some funeral ark and bade farewell by a lunatic blind Noah, all teeth and no tongue, brandishing a pitchfork and fouling the air.

So all stood aside as the flood of shadow and cloud and rain that talked in voices filled the cellar, stashed itself in bins marked with the years they had died but to rise again, and the parlor chairs were seated with aunts and uncles with odd genetics and the kitchen crone had helpers who walked more strangely than she, as more aberrant cousins and long-lost nephews and peculiar nieces shambled or stalked or flew into pavanes about the ceiling chandeliers and feeling the rooms fill below and the grand concourse of unnatural survivals of the unfit, as it was later put, made the pictures tilt on the walls, the mouse run wild in the flues as Egyptian smokes sank, and the spider on Timothy's neck take refuge in his ear, crying an unheard "sanctuary" as Timothy ducked in and stood admiring Cecy, this slumberous marshal of the tumult, and then leaped to see Great

Grandmère, linens bursting with pride, her lapis lazuli eyes all enflamed, and then falling downstairs amidst heartbeats and bombardments of sounds as if he fell through an immense birdcage where were locked an aviary of midnight creatures all wing hastening to arrive but ready to leave until at last with a great roar and a concussion of thunder where there had been no lightning the last storm cloud shut like a lid upon the moonlit roof, the windows, one by one, crashed shut, the doors slammed, the sky was cleared, the roads empty.

And Timothy amidst it all, stunned, gave a great shout of delight.

At which a thousand shadows turned. Two thousand Beast eyes burned yellow, green, and sulfurous gold.

And in the roundabout centrifuge, Timothy with mindless joy was hurled by the whirl and spin to be flung against a wall and held fast by the concussion, where, motionless, forlorn, he could only watch the carousel of shapes and sizes of mist and fog and smoke faces and legs with hooves that, jounced, struck sparks as someone peeled him off the wall in jolts! "Well, you *must* be Timothy! Yes, yes! Hands too warm. Face and cheeks too hot. Brow perspiring. Haven't perspired in years. What's this?" A snarled and hairy fist pummeled Timothy's chest. "Is that a small heart? Hammering like an anvil? Yes?"

A bearded face scowled down at him.

"Yes," said Timothy.

"Poor lad, none of that now, we'll soon stop it!"

And to roars of laughter the chilly hand and the cold moon face lurched away in the roundabout dance.

"That," said Mother, suddenly near, "was your Uncle Jason."

"I don't like him," whispered Timothy.

"You're not supposed to like, son, not supposed to like anyone. It's not in the cards, as they say. He directs funerals."

"Why," said Timothy, "does he have to direct them when there's only one place to *go*?"

"Well said! He needs an apprentice!"

"Not me," said Timothy.

"Not you," said Mother instantly. "Now light more candles. Pass the wine." She handed him a salver on which stood six goblets, brimmed.

"It's not wine, Mother."

"Better than wine. Do you or do you not want to be like us, Timothy?"

"Yes. No. Yes. No."

Crying out, he let the stuff fall to the floor and fled to the front door to fall out in the night.

Where a thunderous avalanche of wings fell down to clout his face, his arms, his hands. A vast confusion brushed his ears, banged his eyes, chopped his upraised fists as, in the terrible roar of this downfell burial he saw a dreadfully smiling face and cried, "Einar! Uncle!"

"Or even Uncle Einar!" shouted the face, and seizing him, threw him high in the night air where, suspended and shrieking, he was caught again as the man with wings leaped up to catch and whirl him, laughing.

"How did you know who I was?" cried the man.

"There's only one uncle with wings," Timothy gasped as they shot above the rooftops, rushed the iron gargoyles, skimmed the shingles and veered up for views of farmlands east and west, north and south.

"Fly, Timothy, fly!" shouted the great bat-winged uncle.

"I am, I am!" gasped Timothy.

"No, really *fly!*"

And laughing, the good uncle tossed and Timothy fell, flapping his arms, and still fell, shrieking, to be caught again.

"Well, well, in time!" said Uncle Einar. "Think. Wish. And with the wishing: *make!*"

Timothy shut his eyes, floating amidst the great flutter of pinions that filled the sky and blinded the stars. He felt small buds of fire in his shoulder blades and wished more and felt bumps grow and push to burst! Hell and damn. Damn and hell!

"In time," said Uncle Einar, guessing his thought. "One day, or you're not my nephew! Quick!"

They skimmed the roof, peered into attic dunes where Cecy dreamed, seized an October wind that soared them to the clouds, and plummeted down, gently, to land upon the porch where two dozen shadows with mist for eyes welcomed them with a proper tumult and rainfall applause.

"Good flying, aye, Timothy?" the uncle shouted, he never murmured, everything was an outrageous explosion, an opera bombardment. "Enough?"

"Enough!" Timothy wept with delight. "Oh, Uncle, thanks."

"His first lesson," Uncle Einar announced. "Soon the air, the sky, the clouds, will be his as well as mine!"

More rainfall applause as Einar carried Timothy in to the dancing phantoms at the tables and the almost-skeletons at the feast. Smokes exhaled from the chimneys shapeless to assume shapes of remembered nephews and cousins, then ceased being smolders and took on flesh to be crushed in the orchestra of dancers and crowd the banquet spreads. Until a cock crowed on some distant farm. All stiffened as if struck. The wildness stilled. The smokes and mists and rain-shapes melted along the cellar steps to stash, lounge, and occupy the bins and boxes with brass-labeled lids. Uncle Einar, last of all, kettledrummed the air

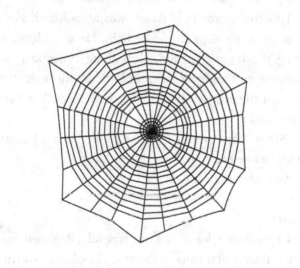

as he descended, laughing at some half-remembered death, perhaps his own, until he lay in the longest box of all and let his wings simmer to be tucked on each side of his laughs and with the last bat-web pinion safely appliquéd to his chest, shut his eyes, gave a nod, and the lid, so summoned, shut down on his laughs as if he were still in flight and the cellar was all silence and dark.

Timothy, in the cold dawn, was abandoned. For all were gone, all slept fearful of light. He was alone, and loving the day and the sun, but wishing somehow to love darkness and night as he crept back up through all the stairs of the House saying, "I'm tired, Cecy. But I can't sleep. Can't."

"Sleep," murmured Cecy, as he lay on the Egyptian sands beside her. "Hear me. Sleep. Sleep."

And, obeying, he slept.

Sunset.

Three dozen long, hollow box-lids slammed wide. Three dozen filaments, cobwebs, ectoplasms swarmed up to pulsate and then—become. Three dozen cousins, nephews, aunts, uncles melted themselves from the vibrant air, a nose here, a mouth here, a set of ears, some upraised hands and gesticulant fingers, waiting for legs to extend the feet to extrude, whereupon they stepped out and down on the cellar floor even as the strange casks popped wide to let forth not vintages but autumn leaves like wings and wings like autumn leaves which stormed footless up the stairs, while from down the vacuumed chimney flues blown forth in cindered smokes, tunes sounded from players invisible, and a rodent of incredible size chorded the piano and waited on applause.

In the midst of which, Timothy was ricocheted from beast-child to dread relative in a volcanic roar so that at last, defeated, he yanked himself free and fled to the kitchen where something huddled against the flooded windowpanes. It sighed and wept and tapped continually, and suddenly he was outside, staring in, the rain beating, the wind chilling him, and all the candle darkness inside lost. Waltzes were being waltzed; he could not waltz. Foods were being devoured he could not devour, wines were being drunk he could not drink.

Timothy shivered and ran upstairs to the moonlit sands and the dunes shaped like ladies and Cecy asleep in their midst.

"Cecy," he called, softly. "Where are you tonight?"

She said, "Far west. California. By a salt sea, near the mud pots and the steam and the quiet. I'm a farmer's wife sitting on a wooden porch. The sun's going down."

"What else, Cecy?"

"You can hear the mud pots whispering," she replied. "The mud pots lift little gray heads of steam, and the heads rip like rubber and collapse with a noise like wet lips. And there is a smell of sulfur and deep burning and old time. The dinosaur has been cooking here two billion years."

"Is he done yet, Cecy?"

Cecy's calm sleeper's lips smiled. "Quite done. Now it's full night here between the mountains. I'm inside this woman's head, looking out through the little holes in her skull, listening to the silence. Planes fly like pterodactyls on huge wings. Further over, a steam shovel Tyrannosaurus stares at those loud reptiles flying high. I watch and smell the smells of prehistoric cookings. Quiet, quiet . . ."

"How long will you stay in her head, Cecy?"

"Until I've listened and looked and felt enough to change her life. Living in her isn't like living anywhere in the world. Her valley with her small wooden house is a dawn world. Black mountains enclose it with silence. Once in half an hour I see a car go by, shining its headlights on a small dirt road, and then silence and night. I sit on the porch all day, and watch the shadows run out from the trees, and join in one big night. I wait for my husband to come home. He never will. The valley, the sea, few cars, the porch, rocking chair, myself, the silence."

"What *now*, Cecy?"

"I'm walking off the porch, toward the mud pots. Now the sulfur fumes are all around. A bird flies over, crying. I'm *in* that bird! And as I fly, inside my new small glass-bead eyes, I see that woman, below, take two steps out into the mud pots! I hear a sound as if a boulder has been dropped! I see a white hand, sinking in a pool of mud. The mud seals over. Now, I'm flying home!"

Something banged against the attic window.

Cecy blinked.

"Now!" she laughed. "I'm *here*!"

Cecy let her eyes wander to find Timothy.

"Why are you upstairs instead of with the Homecoming?"

"Oh, Cecy!" he burst out. "I want to do something to make them see me, make me as fine as them, something to make me belong, and I thought *you* might—"

"Yes," she murmured. "Stand straight! Now, shut your eyes and think nothing, *nothing*!"

He stood very straight and thought of nothing.

She sighed. "Timothy? Ready? Set?"

Like a hand into a glove, Cecy thrust in both ears. "Go!"

"Everyone! Look!"

Timothy lifted the goblet of strange red wine, the pe-

71

culiar vintage, so all could see. Aunts, uncles, cousins, nieces, nephews!

He drank it down.

He waved at his stepsister Laura, held her gaze, to freeze her in place.

Timothy pinned Laura's arms behind her, whispering. Gently, he bit her neck!

Candles blew out. Wind applauded the roof shingles. Aunts and uncles gasped.

Turning, Timothy crammed toadstools in his mouth, swallowed, then beat his arms against his hips and ran in circles. "Uncle Einar! Now I'll *fly!*"

At the top of the stairs, flapping, Timothy heard his mother cry, "No!"

"Yes!" Timothy hurled himself out, thrashing!

Halfway his wings exploded. Screaming, he fell.

To be caught by Uncle Einar.

Timothy squirmed wildly as a voice burst from his lips.

"This is Cecy!" it cried. "Cecy! Come see! In the attic!" Laughter. Timothy tried to stop his mouth.

Laughter. Einar let him drop. Running through the mob as they rushed up toward Cecy, Timothy kicked the front door wide and . . .

Flap! went the wine and toadstools, out into the cold autumn night.

* * *

"Cecy, I hate you, hate you!"

Inside the barn, in deep shadow, Timothy sobbed bitterly and thrashed in a stack of odorous hay. Then he lay still. From his blouse pocket, from the protection of the matchbox used as his retreat, the spider crawled forth and along Timothy's shoulder to his neck to climb to his ear.

Timothy trembled. "No, no. Don't!"

The delicate touch of the feeler on his tympanum, small signals of large concern, made Timothy's crying cease.

The spider then traveled down his cheek, stationed itself beneath his nose, probing the nostrils as if to seek the melancholy in there, and then moved quietly up over the rim of his nose to sit, peering at Timothy, until he burst with laughter.

"Get, Arach! *Go!*"

In answer, the spider floated down and with sixteen delicate motions wove its filaments zigzag over Timothy's mouth which could only sound:

"Mmmmmm!"

Timothy sat up, rustling the hay.

Mouse was there in his blouse pocket, a small snug contentment to touch his chest and heart.

Anuba was there, curled in a soft round ball of sleep, all adream with many fine fish swimming in freshets of dream.

The land was painted with moonlight now. In the big House he could hear the ribald laughter as "Mirror, Mirror" was played with a huge mirror. Celebrants roared as they tried to identify those of themselves whose reflections did not, had not *ever,* and *never would* appear in a glass.

Timothy broke Arach's web on his lips:

"Now what?"

Falling to the floor, Arach scuttled swiftly toward the House, until Timothy trapped and tucked him back in his ear. "All right. Here we go, for fun, no matter what!"

He ran. Behind, Mouse ran small, Anuba large. Half across the yard, a green tarpaulin fell from the sky and pinned him flat with silken wing. "Uncle!"

"Timothy." Einar's wings clamored like kettledrums. Timothy, a thimble, was set on Einar's shoulder. "Cheer up, nephew. How much richer things are for you. Our world is dead. All tombstone-gray. Life's best to those who live least, worth more per ounce, more per ounce!"

From midnight on, Uncle Einar soared him about the House, from room to room, weaving, singing, as they fetched A Thousand Times Great Grandmère down, wrapped in her Egyptian cerements, roll on roll of linen bandage coiled about her fragile archaeopteryx bones.

Silently she stood, stiff as a great loaf of Nile bread, her eyes flinting a wise, silent fire. At the predawn breakfast, she was propped at the head of the long table and suffered sips of incredible wines to wet her dusty mouth.

The wind rose, the stars burned, the dances quickened. The many darknesses roiled, bubbled, vanished, reappeared.

"Coffins" was next. Coffins, in a row, surrounded by marchers, timed to a flute. One by one coffins were removed. The scramble for their polished interiors eliminated two, four, six, eight marchers, until one coffin remained. Timothy circled it cautiously with his fey-cousin, Rob. The flute stopped. Gopher to hole, Timothy lunged at the box. Rob popped in first! Applause!

Laughter and chat.

"How is Uncle Einar's sister? She of the wings."

"Lotte flew over Persia last week and was shot with arrows. A bird for a banquet. A bird!"

Their laughter was a cave of winds.

"And Carl?"

"The one who lives under bridges? Poor Carl. No place in all Europe for him. New bridges are rebuilt with Holy Water blessings! Carl is homeless. There are refugees tonight beyond counting."

"True! *All* the bridges, eh? Poor Carl."

"Listen!"

The party held still. Far off, a town clock chimed 6 A.M. The Homecoming was done. In time with the clock striking, a hundred voices began to sing songs that were centuries old. Uncles and aunts twined their arms around each other, circling, singing, and somewhere in the cold distance of morning the town clock stopped its chimes and was still.

Timothy sang.

He knew no words, no tune, yet he sang and the words and tune were pure, round and high and beautiful.

Finished, he gazed up to the High Attic of Egyptian sands and dreams.

"Thanks, Cecy," he whispered.

A wind blew. Her voice echoed from his mouth, "Do you forgive me?"

Then he said, "Cecy. Forgiven."

Then he relaxed and let his mouth move as it wished, and the song continued, rhythmically, purely, melodiously.

Goodbyes were said in a great rustling. Mother and Father stood in grave happiness at the door to kiss each departing cheek. The sky, beyond, colored and shone in the east. A cold wind entered. They must all rise and fly west to beat the sun around the world. Make haste, oh, make haste!

Again Timothy listened to a voice in his head and said, "Yes, Cecy. I would like that. Thanks."

And Cecy helped him into one body after another. Instantly, he felt himself inside an ancient cousin's body at the door, bowing and pressing lips to Mother's pale fingers, looking out at her from a wrinkled leather face. Then he stepped out into a wind that seized and blew him in a flurry of leaves away up over the awakening hills.

With a snap, Timothy was behind another face, at the door, all farewells. It was Cousin William's face.

Cousin William, swift as smoke, loped down a dirt road, red eyes burning, fur pelt rimed with morning, padded feet falling with silent sureness, panting over a hill into a hollow, and then suddenly in flight, flying away.

Then Timothy welled up in the tall umbrella shape of Uncle Einar to look out from his wildly amused eyes as he picked up a tiny pale body: *Timothy!* Picking up *himself!* "Be a good boy, Timothy. See you soon!"

Swifter than borne leaves, with a webbed thunder of wings, faster than the lupine thing of the country road, going so swiftly the earth's features blurred and the last stars tilted, like a pebble in Uncle Einar's mouth, Timothy flew, joined on half his flight.

Then slammed back in his own flesh.

The shouting and the laughing faded and were almost lost. Everybody was embracing and crying and thinking how the world was becoming less a place for them. There had been a time when they had met every year, but now decades passed with no reconciliation. "Don't forget, we meet in Salem in 2009!" someone cried.

Salem. Timothy's numbed mind touched the word. Salem—2009. And there would be Uncle Fry and Grandma and Grandfather and A Thousand Times Great Grandmère in her withered cerements. And Mother and Father and Cecy and all the rest. But would *he* be alive that long?

With one last withering wind blast, away they all shot, so many scarves, so many fluttery mammals, so many seared leaves, so many wolves loping, so many whinings and clusterings, so many midnights and dawns and sleeps and wakenings.

Mother shut the door.

Father walked down into the cellar.

Timothy walked across the crepe-littered hall. His head was down, and in passing the party mirror he saw the pale mortality of his face. He shivered.

"Timothy," said Mother.

She laid a hand on his face. "Son," she said. "We love you. We all love you. No matter how different you are, no matter if you leave us one day." She kissed his cheek.

"And if and when you die your bones will lie undisturbed, we'll see to that, you'll lie at ease forever, and I'll come see you every All Hallows' Eve and tuck you in more secure."

The halls echoed to polished lids creaking and slamming shut.

The House was silent. Far away, the wind went over a hill with its last cargo of small dark flights, echoing, chittering.

He walked up the steps, one by one, crying to himself all the way.

CHAPTER 10

West of October

The four cousins—Peter, William, Philip, and Jack—had lingered on after the Homecoming because a cloud of doom and melancholy and disbelief hung over Europe. There was no room in the dark House, so they were stashed almost upside-down in the barn, which shortly thereafter burned.

Like most of the Family they were not ordinary.

To say that most of them slept days and worked at odd occupations nights would fall short of commencement.

To remark that some of them could read minds, and some fly with lightnings to land with leaves, would be an understatement.

To add that some could not be seen in mirrors while others could be found in multitudinous shapes, sizes, and textures in the same glass would merely repeat gossip that veered into truth.

These boys resembled their uncles, aunts, cousins, and grandparents by the toadstool score and the mushroom dozen.

They were just about every color you could mix in one restless night.

Some were young and others had been around since the Sphinx first sank its stone paws in tidal sands.

And all four were in love and in need for one special Family member.

Cecy.

Cecy. She was the reason, the real reason, the central reason for the wild cousins to circle her and stay. For she was as seedpod full as a pomegranate. She was all the senses of all the creatures in the world. She was all the motion-picture houses and stage-play theaters and all the art galleries of all time.

Ask her to yank your soul like an aching tooth and shoot it into clouds to cool your spirit, and yanked you were, drawn high to drift in the mists.

Ask her to seize that same soul and bind it in the flesh of a tree, and you awoke the next morning with birds singing in your green head.

Ask to be pure rain and you fell on everything. Ask to be the moon and suddenly you looked down to see your pale light painting lost towns the color of tombstones and spectral ghosts.

Cecy. Who extracted your soul and pulled forth your impacted wisdom, and could transfer it to animal, vegetable, or mineral; name your poison.

No wonder the cousins lingered.

And along about sunset, before the dreadful fire, they climbed to the attic to stir her bed of Egyptian sands with their breath.

"Well," said Cecy, eyes shut, a smile playing about her mouth. "What would your pleasure be?"

"I—" said Peter.

"Maybe—" said William and Philip.

"Could you—" said Jack.

"Take you on a visit to the local insane asylum," guessed Cecy, "to peek inside people's corkscrew heads?"

"Yes!"

"Done!" said Cecy. "Go lie on your cots in the barn. Over, up, and—out!"

Like corks, their souls popped. Like birds, they flew. Like bright needles, they shot in various crazed asylum ears.

"Ah!" they cried in delight.

Good Times
Bad Times
all Times
get over

While they were gone, the barn burned.

In all the shouting and confusion, the running for water, the general ramshackle hysteria, everyone forgot who was in the barn or what the high-flying cousins and Cecy, asleep, might be up to. So deep in her rushing dreams was she, that she felt neither the flames, nor the dread moment when the walls fell and four human-shaped torches self-destroyed. A clap of thunder banged across country, shook the skies, knocked the wind-blown essences of cousins through mill-fans, while Cecy, with a gasp, sat straight up and gave one shriek that shot the cousins home. All four, at the moment of concussion, had been in various asylum bins, prying trapdoor skulls to peek in at maelstroms of confetti the colors of madness, the dark rainbows of nightmare.

"What happened?" cried Jack from Cecy's mouth.

"What!" said Philip, moving her lips.

"My god." William stared from her eyes.

"The barn burned," said Peter. "We're lost!"

The Family, soot-faced in the smoking yard, turned like a traveling minstrel's funeral and stared up at Cecy in shock.

"Cecy?" called Mother, wildly. "Is someone *with* you?"

"Me, Peter!" shouted Peter from her lips.

"Philip!"

"William!"

"Jack!"

The souls counted off from Cecy's tongue.

The Family waited.

Then, as one, the four young men's voices asked the final, most dreadful question:

"Didn't you save just *one* body?"

The Family sank an inch into the earth, burdened with a reply they could not give.

"But—" Cecy held on to her elbows, touched her own chin, her mouth, her brow, inside which four live ghosts wrestled for room. "But—what'll I *do* with them?" Her eyes searched all those faces below in the yard. "My cousins can't stay! They can't stand around in my *head*!"

What she cried after that, or what the cousins babbled, crammed like pebbles under her tongue, or what the Family said, running like burned chickens in the yard, was lost.

With Judgment Day thunders, the rest of the barn fell.

With a vast whisper the ashes blew away in an October wind that leaned this way and that on the attic roof.

"It seems to me," said Father.

"Not seems, but *is*!" said Cecy, eyes shut.

"We must farm the cousins out. Find temporary hospices until such time as we can cull new bodies—"

"The quicker the better," said four voices from Cecy's mouth, now high, now low, now two gradations between.

Father continued in darkness. "There must be *someone* in the Family with a small room in the backside of their cerebellum! Volunteers!"

The Family sucked in an icy breath and stayed silent. Great Grandmère, far above in her own attic place, suddenly whispered: "I hereby solicit, name, and nominate the oldest of the old!"

As if their heads were on a single string, everyone turned to blink at a far corner where their ancient Nile River Grandpère leaned like a dry bundle of two-millennia-before-Christ wheat.

The Nile ancestor husked, "No!"

"Yes!" Grandmère shut her sand-slit eyes, folded her brittle arms over her tomb-painted bosom. "You have all the time in the world."

"Again, no!" The mortuary wheat rustled.

"This," Grandmère murmured, "is the Family, all strange-fine. We walk nights, fly winds and airs, wander storms, read minds, work magic, live forever or a thousand years, whichever. In sum, we're Family, to be leaned on, turned to, when—"

"No, no!"

"Hush." One eye as large as the Star of India opened, burned, dimmed, died. "It's not proper, four wild men in a slim girl's head. And there's much *you* can teach the cousins. You thrived long before Napoleon walked in and ran *out* of Russia, or Ben Franklin died of pox. Fine if the boys' souls were lodged in *your* ear some while. It might straighten their spines. Would you deny this?"

The ancient ancestor from the White and Blue Niles gave only the faintest percussion of harvest wreaths.

"Well, then," said the frail remembrance of Pharaoh's daughter. "Children of the nigh, did you hear!?"

"We heard!" cried the ghosts from Cecy's mouth.

"Move!" said the four-thousand-year-old mummification.

"We move!" said the four.

And since no one had bothered to say which cousin went first, there was a surge of phantom tissue, a tide-drift of storm on the unseen wind.

Four different expressions lit Grandpère's harvest ancestor's face. Four earthquakes shook his brittle frame. Four smiles ran scales along his yellow piano teeth. Before he could protest, at four different gaits and speeds, he was shambled from the house, across the lawn, and down the lost railroad tracks toward town, a mob of laughter in his cereal throat.

The Family leaned from the porch, staring after the rushing parade of one.

Cecy, deep asleep again, gaped her mouth to free the echoes of the mob.

At noon the next day the big, dull-blue iron engine panted into the railroad station to find the Family restless on the platform, the old harvest pharaoh supported in their midst. They not so much walked but carried him to the day coach, which smelled of fresh varnish and hot plush. Along the way, the Nile traveler, eyes shut, uttered curses in many voices that everyone ignored.

They propped him like an ancient corn-shock in his seat, fastened a hat on his head like putting a new roof on an old building, and addressed his wrinkled face.

"Grandpère, sit up. Grandpère, are you *in* there? Get out of the way, cousins, let the old one speak."

"Here." His dry mouth twitched and whistled. "And suffering *their* sins and misery! Oh, damn, damn!"

"No!" "Lies!" "We did nothing!" cried the voices from one side, then the other, of his mouth. "Cease!"

"Silence!" Father seized the ancient chin and focused the inner bones with a shake. "West of October is Sojourn, Missouri, not a long trip. We have kin there. Uncles, aunts, some with, some without children. Since Cecy's mind can only travel a few miles, you must cargo-

89

transit these obstreperous cousins yet farther and stash them with Family flesh and minds."

"But if you can't distribute the fools," he added, "bring them back alive."

"Goodbye!" said four voices from the ancient harvest bundle.

"Goodbye Grandpère, Peter, William, Philip, Jack!"

"Forget me not!" a young woman's voice cried.

"Cecy!" all shouted. "Farewell!"

The train chanted away, west of October.

The train rounded a long curve. The Nile ancestor leaned and creaked.

"Well," whispered Peter, "here we are."

"Yes." William went on: "Here we are."

The train whistled.

"Tired," said Jack.

"*You're* tired!" the ancient one rasped.

"Stuffy in here," said Philip.

"Expect that! The ancient one is four thousand years old, right, old one? Your skull is a tomb."

"Cease!" The old one gave his own brow a thump. A panic of birds knocked in his head. "Cease!"

"There," whispered Cecy, quieting the panic. "I've slept well and I'll come for *part* of the trip, Grandpère, to teach you how to hold, stay, and keep the resident crows and vultures in your cage."

"Crows! Vultures!" the cousins protested.

"Silence," said Cecy, tamping the cousins like tobacco in an ancient uncleaned pipe. Far away, her body lay on her Egyptian sands, but her mind circled, touched, pushed, enchanted, kept. "Enjoy. Look!"

The cousins looked.

And indeed, wandering in the upper keeps of the ancient tomb was like surviving in a dim sarcophagus in which memories, transparent wings folded, lay piled in ribboned bundles, in files, packets, shrouded figures, strewn shadows. Here and there, a special bright memory, like a single ray of amber light, struck in upon and shaped a golden hour, a summer day. There was a smell of worn leather and burnt horsehair and the faintest scent of uric acid from the jaundiced stones that ached about them as they jostled half-seen elbows.

"Look," murmured the cousins. "Oh, yes! Yes!"

For now, quietly indeed, they were peering through the dusty panes of the ancient's eyes, viewing the great hellfire train that bore them and the green-turning-to-brown autumn world streaming, passing as before a house with cobwebbed windows. When they worked the old one's mouth it was like ringing a lead clapper in a rusted bell. The sounds of the world wandered in through his hollow ears, static on a badly tuned radio.

"Still," Peter said, "it's better than having no body at all."

The train banged across a bridge in thunders.

"Think I'll look around," said Peter.

The ancient felt his limbs stir.

"Stay! Lie back! Sit!"

The old one crammed his eyes tight.

"Open up! Let's see!"

His eyeballs swiveled.

"Here comes a lovely girl. Quick!"

"Most beautiful girl in the *world!*"

The mummy couldn't help but peel one eye.

"Ah!" said everyone. *"Right!"*

The young woman curved, leaning as the train pushed or pulled her; as pretty as something you won at a carnival by knocking over milk bottles.

"No!" The old one slammed his lids.

"Open wide!"

His eyeballs churned.

"Let go!" he shouted. "Stop!"

The young woman lurched as if to fall on *all* of them.

"Stop!" cried the old, old person. "Cecy's with us, all innocence."

"Innocence!" The inner attic roared.

"Grandpère," said Cecy softly. "With all my nigh excursions, my traveling, I am not—"

"Innocent!" the four cousins shouted.

"Look here!" protested Grandpère.

"*You* look," whispered Cecy. "I have sewn my way through bedroom windows on a thousand summer nights. I have lain in cool snowbeds of white pillows and swum unclothed in rivers on August noons to lie on riverbeds for birds to see—"

"I will not listen!"

"Yes." Cecy's voice wandered in meadows of remembrance. "I have lingered in a girl's summer face to look out at a young man, and I have been in that same man, the same instant, breathing fire at that forever summer girl. I have nested in mating mice, circling lovebirds, bleeding-heart doves, and hid in butterflies fused on a flower."

"Damn!"

"I've run in sleighs on December midnights when snow fell and smoke plumed out of the horses' pink nostrils and there were fur blankets piled high with six young people hidden warm, delving, wishing, finding—"

"Cease!"

"Brava!" yelled the cousins.

"—and I have lodged in an edifice of bone and flesh— the most beautiful woman in the world . . ."

Grandpère was stunned.

For now it was as if snow fell to quiet him. He felt a stir of flowers about his brow, and a blowing of July morning wind about his ears, and all through his limbs a burgeoning of warmth, a growth of bosom about his ancient flat chest, a fire struck to bloom in the pit of his stomach. Now, as she talked, his lips softened and colored and knew poetry and might have let it pour forth in incredible rains, and his worn and tomb-dust fingers tumbled in his lap and changed to cream and milk and melting apple-snow. He stared down at them, frozen, and clenched his fists.

"No! Give back my hands! Cleanse my mouth!"

"Enough," said an inner voice, Philip.

"We're wasting time," said Peter.

"Let's *greet* the young lady," said Jack.

"Aye!" said the Mormon Tabernacle Choir from a single throat. Grandpère was yanked to his feet by unseen wires.

"Let me be!" he cried, and vised his eyes, his skull, his ribs, an incredible strange bed that sank to smother the cousins. "There! Stop!"

The cousins ricocheted in the dark.

"Help! Light! Cecy!"

"Here," said Cecy.

The old one felt himself twitched, tickled, behind his

ears, his spine. His lungs filled with feathers, his nose sneezed soot.

"Will, his left leg, move! Peter, the right, step! Philip, right arm. Jack, the left. Fling!"

"Double-time. Run!"

Grandpère lurched.

But he didn't lurch at the fine girl; he swayed and half collapsed away.

"Wait!" cried the Greek chorus. "She's back there! Someone trip him. Who has his legs? Will? Peter?"

Grandpère flung the vestibule door wide, fell out on the windy platform and was about to hurl himself full into a meadow of swiftly flashing sunflowers when:

"Statues!" said the chorus stuffed in his mouth.

And statue he became on the backside of the swiftly vanishing train.

Spun about, Grandpère found himself back inside. As the train rocketed a curve, he sat on a young lady's hands.

"Excuse!" Grandpère leaped up.

"Excused." She rearranged her hands.

"No trouble, no, no!" The old, old creature collapsed on the seat across from her. "Hell! Bats, back in the belfry! Damn!"

The cousins melted the wax in his ears.

"Remember," he hissed behind his teeth, "while

you're acting young in there, I'm Tut, fresh from the tomb out here."

"But—" The chamber quartet fiddled his lids. "We'll *make* you young!"

They lit a fuse in his belly, a bomb in his chest.

"No!"

Grandpère yanked a cord. A trapdoor gaped. The cousins fell down into an endless maze of blazing remembrance: three-dimensional shapes as rich and warm as the girl across the aisle. The cousins fell.

"Watch out!"

"I'm lost!"

"Peter?"

"I'm somewhere in Wisconsin. How'd I get *here*?"

"*I'm* on a Hudson River boat. William?"

Far off, William called, "London. My god! Newspapers say the date's August twenty-second, 1800!"

"Cecy?! *You* did this!"

"No, me!" Grandpère shouted everywhere, all about. "You're still in my ears, damn, but living my old times and places. Mind your heads!"

"Hold on!" said William. "Is this the Grand Canyon or your medulla oblongata?"

"Grand Canyon. Nineteen twenty-one."

"A woman!" cried Peter. "Here before me."

And indeed this woman was beautiful as the spring,

two hundred years ago. Grandpère recalled no name. She had been someone passing with wild strawberries on a summer noon.

Peter reached for the fabulous ghost.

"Away!" shouted Grandpère.

And the girl's face exploded in the summer air and vanished down the road.

"Blast!" cried Peter.

His brothers rampaged, breaking the doors, lifting windows.

"My god! Look!" they shouted.

For Grandpère's memories lay side by side, neat as sardines, a million deep, a million wide, stashed by seconds, minutes, hours. Here a dark girl brushing her hair. There a blond girl running, or asleep. All trapped in honeycombs the color of their summer cheeks. Their smiles flashed. You could pluck them up, turn them round, send them off, call them back. Cry "Italy, 1797," and they danced through warm pavilions, or swam in firefly tides.

"Grandpère, does Grandmère know about these?"

"There are more!"

"Thousands!"

Grandpère flung back a tissue of remembrance. "Here!"

A thousand women wandered a labyrinth.

"Bravo, Grandpère!"

From ear to ear, he felt them rummage cities, alleys, rooms.

Until Jack seized one lone and lovely lady.

"Got you!"

She turned.

"Fool!" she whispered.

The lovely woman's flesh burned away. The chin grew gaunt, the cheeks hollow, the eyes sank.

"Grandmère, it's *you*!"

"Four thousand years ago," she murmured.

"Cecy!" Grandpère raged. "Stash Jack in a dog, a tree! Anywhere but my damn fool head!"

"Out, Jack!" commanded Cecy.

And Jack was out.

Left in a robin on a pole flashing by.

Grandmère stood withered in darkness. Grandpère's inward gaze touched to reclothe her younger flesh. New color filled her eyes, cheeks, and hair. He put her safely away in an orchard of trees in Alexandria when time was new.

Grandpère opened his eyes.

Sunlight blinded the remaining cousins.

The maiden still sat across the aisle.

The cousins jumped behind his gaze.

"Fools!" they said. "Why bother with *old*? New is *now*!"

"Yes," whispered Cecy. "Now! I'll tuck Grandpère's mind in *her* body and bring her dreams to hide in his head. He will sit ramrod straight. Inside him we'll all be acrobats, gymnasts, fiends! The conductor will pass, not guessing. Grandpère's head will fill with wild laughter, unclothed mobs, while his true mind will be trapped in that fine girl's brow. What fun on a train on a hot afternoon!"

"Yes!" everyone shouted.

"No." And Grandpère pulled forth two white tablets and swallowed.

"Stop!"

"Drat!" said Cecy. "It was such a fine, wicked plan."

"Goodnight, sleep well," said Grandpère. "And you—" He gazed with gentle sleepiness at the maiden across the aisle. "You have just been saved from a fate, young lady, worse than four male cousins' deaths."

"Pardon?"

"Innocence, continue in thy innocence," murmured Grandpère, and fell asleep.

The train pulled into Sojourn, Missouri, at six. Only then was Jack allowed back from his exile in the head of that robin of a faraway tree.

There were absolutely no relatives in Sojourn willing to put up with the rampant cousins, so Grandpère rode the train back to Illinois, the cousins ripe in him, like peach stones.

And there they stayed, each in a different territory of Grandpère's sun- or moonlit attic keep.

Peter took up residence in a remembrance of 1840 in Vienna with a crazed actress; William lived in the Lake Country with a flaxen-haired Swede of some indefinite years; while Jack shuttled from fleshpot to fleshpot—Frisco, Berlin, Paris—appearing, on occasion, as a wicked glitter in Grandpère's eyes. And Philip, all wise, locked himself deep in a library cell to con all the books that Grandpère loved.

But on some nights Grandpère edges over through the attic toward Grandmère, no four thousand, now fourteen, years old.

"You! At *your* age!" she shrieks.

And she flails and flails him until, laughing in five voices, Grandpère gives up, falls back, and pretends to sleep, alert with five kinds of alertness, ready for another try.

Perhaps in four thousand years.

Many Returns

Incredibly, what went up had to come down.

In a blizzard of darkness all over the world, the winds blew backward, and what stormed up hesitated on the verge of the horizon and then fell back upon the continent of America.

All over upper Illinois storm clouds gathered and began to rain, and they rained souls and they rained departed wings and they rained tears from people who had to give up traveling and return to the Homecoming and were sad instead of glad.

All over the skies of Europe and the skies of America what had been a happy occasion was now melancholy, driven back by clouds of oppression and prejudice and disbelief. The inhabitants of the Homecoming returned to the threshold of the House and slid in through the windows, the garrets, the cellars, and hid away fast to astound the Family who wondered, how come? A second Homecoming? Was the world coming to an end? And yes, it was, their world, anyway. This rain of souls, this storm of lost people, clustered on the roof, brimmed the basement among the wine kegs, and waited for some sort of revelation, which then caused the members of the Family to decide to meet in council and welcome one by one those people who needed to be hidden from the world.

And the first of these strange lost souls was in a train traveling north through Europe, traveling north toward fogs and mists and to fine and nourishing rains . . .

CHAPTER 12

On the Orient North

It was on the Orient Express heading away from Venice to Paris to Calais that the old woman noticed the ghastly passenger.

He was a traveler obviously dying of some dread disease.

He occupied compartment 22 on the third car back and had his meals sent in, and only at twilight did he rouse to come sit in the dining car surrounded by the false electric lights and the sound of tinkling crystal and women's laughter.

He arrived this night, moving with a terrible slowness, to sit across the aisle from this woman of some years, her bosom like a fortress, her brow serene, her eyes filled with a kindness that had mellowed with time.

There was a black medical bag at her side, and a thermometer tucked in her mannish lapel pocket.

The ghastly man's paleness caused her left hand to crawl up along her lapel to touch the thermometer.

"Oh, dear," whispered Miss Minerva Halliday.

The maître d' was passing. She touched his elbow and nodded across the aisle.

"Pardon, but where is that poor man going?"

"Calais and London, madam. If God is willing."

And he hurried off.

Minerva Halliday, her appetite gone, stared across at that skeleton made of snow.

The man and the cutlery laid before him seemed one. The knives, forks, and spoons jingled with a silvery cold sound. He listened, fascinated, as if to the voice of his inner soul as the cutlery crept, touched, chimed; a tintinnabulation from another sphere. His hands lay in his lap like lonely pets, and when the train swerved around a long curve his body, mindless, swayed now this way, now that, toppling.

At which moment the train took a greater curve and knocked the silverware chittering. A woman at a far table, laughing, cried out: "I don't *believe* it!"

To which a man with a louder laugh shouted:

"Nor do *I!*"

This coincidence caused, in the ghastly passenger, a terrible melting. The doubting laughter had pierced his ears.

He visibly shrank. His eyes hollowed and one could almost imagine a cold vapor gasped from his mouth.

Miss Minerva Halliday, shocked, leaned forward and put out one hand. She heard herself whisper:

"*I* believe!"

The effect was instantaneous.

The ghastly passenger sat up. Color returned to his white cheeks. His eyes glowed with a rebirth of fire. His head swiveled and he stared across the aisle at this miraculous woman with words that cured.

Blushing furiously, the old nurse with the great warm bosom flinched, rose, and hurried off.

Not five minutes later, Miss Minerva Halliday heard the maître d' hurrying along the corridor, tapping on doors, whispering. As he passed her open door, he glanced at her.

"Could it be that you are—"

"No," she guessed, "not a doctor. But a registered nurse. Is it that old man in the dining car?"

"Yes, yes! Please, madam, this way!"

The ghastly man had been carried back to his own compartment.

Reaching it, Miss Minerva Halliday peered within.

And there the strange man lay, his eyes wilted shut, his mouth a bloodless wound, the only life in him the joggle of his head as the train swerved.

My God, she thought, he's *dead*!

Out loud she said, "I'll call if I need you."

The maître d' went away.

Miss Minerva Halliday quietly shut the sliding door and turned to examine the dead man—for surely he was dead. And yet . . .

But at last she dared to reach out and to touch the wrists in which so much ice water ran. She pulled back, as if her fingers had been burned by dry ice. Then she leaned forward to whisper into the pale man's face.

"Listen very carefully. *Yes?*"

For answer, she thought she heard the coldest throb of a single heartbeat.

She continued. "I do not know how I guess this. I know who you are, and what you are sick of—"

The train curved. His head lolled as if his neck had been broken.

"I'll tell you what you're dying from!" she whispered. "You suffer a disease—of *people*!"

His eyes popped wide, as if he had been shot through the heart. She said:

"The people on this train are killing you. *They* are your affliction."

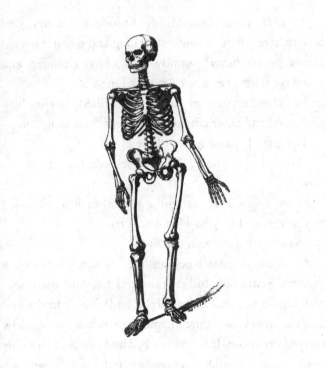

Something like a breath stirred behind the shut wound of the man's mouth.

"Yessss . . . sss."

Her grip tightened on his wrist, probing for some pulse:

"You are from some Middle European country, yes? Somewhere where the nights are long and when the wind blows, people *listen*? But now things have changed, and you have tried to escape by travel, but . . ."

Just then, a party of young, wine-filled tourists bustled along the outer corridor, firing off their laughter.

The ghastly passenger withered.

"How do . . . you . . ." he whispered, ". . . know . . . thisss?"

"I am a special nurse with a special memory. I saw, I met, someone like you when I was six—"

"Saw?" the pale man exhaled.

"In Ireland, near Kileshandra. My uncle's house, a hundred years old, full of rain and fog and there was walking on the roof late at night, and sounds in the hall as if the storm had come in, and then at last this shadow entered my room. It sat on my bed and the cold from his body made *me* cold. I remember and know it was no dream, for the shadow who came to sit on my bed and whisper . . . was much . . . like you."

Eyes shut, from the depths of his arctic soul, the old sick man mourned in response:

"And who . . . and *what* . . . am I?"

"You are not sick. And you are not dying . . . You *are*—"

The whistle on the Orient Express wailed a long way off.

"—a ghost," she said.

"Yessss!" he cried.

It was a vast shout of need, recognition, assurance. He almost bolted upright.

"Yes!"

At which moment there arrived in the doorway a young priest, eager to perform. Eyes bright, lips moist, one hand clutching his crucifix, he stared at the collapsed figure of the ghastly passenger and cried, "May I—?"

"Last rites?" The ancient passenger opened one eye like the lid on a silver box. "From you? No." His eye shifted to the nurse. *"Her!"*

"Sir!" cried the young priest.

He stepped back, seized his crucifix as if it were a parachute ripcord, spun, and scurried off.

Leaving the old nurse to sit examining her now even more strange patient until at last he said:

"How," he gasped, "can *you* nurse *me*?"

"Why—" She gave a small self-deprecating laugh. "We must *find* a way."

With yet another wail, the Orient Express encountered more mileages of night, fog, mist, and cut through it with a shriek.

"You are going to Calais?" she said.

"And beyond, to Dover, London, and perhaps a castle outside Edinburgh, where I will be safe—"

"That's almost impossible—" She might as well have shot him through the heart. "No, no, wait, wait!" she cried. "Impossible . . . without *me*! I will travel with you to Calais and across to Dover."

"But you do not *know* me!"

"Oh, but I dreamed you as a child, long before I met someone like you, in the mists and rains of Ireland. At age nine I searched the moors for the Baskerville Hound."

"Yes," said the ghastly passenger. "You are English and the English *believe*!"

"True. Better than Americans, who *doubt*. French? Cynics! English is best. There is hardly an old London house that does not have its sad lady of mists crying before dawn."

At which moment, the compartment door, shaken by a long curve of track, sprang wide. An onslaught of poisonous talk, of delirious chatter, of what could only be irreligious laughter poured in from the corridor. The ghastly passenger wilted.

Springing to her feet, Minerva Halliday slammed the door and turned to look with the familiarity of a lifetime of sleep-tossed encounters at her traveling companion.

"You, now," she asked, "who exactly are *you*?"

The ghastly passenger, seeing in her face the face of a sad child he might have encountered long ago, now described his life:

"I have 'lived' in one place outside Vienna for two hundred years. To survive, assaulted by atheists as well as true believers, I have hid in libraries, in dust-filled stacks, there to dine on myths and moundyard tales. I have taken midnight feasts of panic and terror from bolting horses, baying dogs, catapulting tomcats ... crumbs shaken from tomb lids. As the years passed, my compatriots of the unseen world vanished one by one as castles tumbled or lords rented out their haunted gardens to women's clubs or bed-and-breakfast entrepreneurs. Evicted, we ghastly wanderers of the world have sunk in tar, bog, and fields of disbelief, doubt, scorn, or outright derision. With the populations and disbeliefs doubling by the day, all of my specter friends have fled. Where, I know not. I am the last, trying to train across Europe to some safe, rain-drenched castle keep where men are properly frightened by soots and smokes of wandering souls. England and Scotland for me!"

His voice faded into silence.

"And your name?" she said, at last.

"I *have* no name," he whispered. "A thousand fogs have visited my family plot. A thousand rains have drenched my tombstone. The chisel marks were erased by mist and water and sun. My name has vanished with the flowers and the grass and the marble dust." He opened his eyes.

"*Why* are you doing this?" he said. "*Helping* me?"

And at last she smiled, for she heard the right answer fall from her lips:

"I have never in my life had a *lark*."

"Lark!?"

"My life was that of a stuffed owl. I was not a nun, yet never married. Treating an invalid mother and a half-blind father, I gave myself to hospitals, tombstone beds, cries at night, and medicines that are not perfume to passing men. So, I am something of a ghost myself, yes? And now, tonight, sixty-six years on, I have at last found in you a *patient*! Magnificently different, fresh, absolutely *new*. Oh, Lord, what a challenge. I will pace you, to face people off the train, through the crowds in Paris, then the trip to the sea, off the train, onto the ferry! It will indeed be a—"

"Lark!" cried the ghastly passenger. Spasms of laughter shook him. "Larks? Yes, *that* is what we are!"

"But," she said, "in Paris, do they not *eat* larks even while they roast priests?"

He shut his eyes and whispered, "Paris? Ah, yes."

The train wailed. The night passed.

And they arrived in Paris.

And even as they arrived, a boy, no more than six, ran past and froze. He stared at the ghastly passenger and the ghastly passenger shot back a remembrance of Antarctic ice floes. The boy gave a cry and fled. The old nurse flung the door wide to peer out.

The boy was gibbering to his father at the far end of the corridor. The father charged along the corridor, crying:

"What goes *on* here? Who has frightened my—?"

The man stopped. Outside the door he now fixed his gaze on this bleak occupant on the slowing braking Orient Express. He braked his own tongue. "—my son."

The ghastly passenger looked at him quietly with fog-gray eyes.

"I—" The Frenchman drew back, sucking his teeth in disbelief. "Forgive me!" he gasped. "Regrets!"

And turned to shove at his son. "Troublemaker. Get!" Their door slammed.

"Paris!" echoed through the train.

"Hush and hurry!" advised Minerva Halliday as she

bustled her ancient friend out onto a platform milling with bad tempers and misplaced luggage.

"I am *melting*!" cried the ghastly passenger.

"Not where *I'm* taking you!" She displayed a picnic hamper and flung him forth to the miracle of a single remaining taxicab. And they arrived under a stormy sky at the Père Lachaise cemetery. The great gates were swinging shut. The nurse waved a handful of francs. The gate froze.

Inside, they wandered off-balance but at peace amongst ten thousand monuments. So much cold marble was there, and so many hidden souls, that the old nurse felt a sudden dizziness, a pain in one wrist, and a swift coldness on the left side of her face. She shook her head, refusing this. And they stumbled on among the stones.

"Where do we picnic?" he said.

"Anywhere," she said. "But carefully! For this is a *French* cemetery! Packed with disbelief. *Armées* of egotists who burned people for their faith one year only to be burned for *their* faith the next! Pick! Choose!" They walked. The ghastly passenger nodded. "This first stone. Beneath it: *nothing*. Death final, not a *whisper* of time. The *second* stone: a woman, a secret believer because she loved her husband and hoped to see him again in eternity . . . a murmur of spirit here, the turning of a heart. *Better*. Now this third gravestone: a writer of thrillers for a French magazine. But he *loved* his nights, his fogs, his castles. *This* stone is a proper temperature, like a good wine. Here we shall sit, dear lady, as you decant the champagne and we wait to catch our train."

She offered a glass. "*Can* you drink?"

"One can try." He took it. "One can only try."

The ghastly passenger almost "died" as they left Paris. A group of intellectuals, fresh from seminars about Sartre's "nausea," and hot-air-ballooning about Simone de Beauvoir, streamed through the corridors, leaving the air behind them boiled and empty.

The pale passenger became paler.

The second stop beyond Paris, another invasion! A group of Germans surged aboard, loud in their disbelief of ancestral spirits, doubtful of politics, some even carrying books titled *Was God Ever Home?*

The Orient ghost sank deeper in his X-ray-image bones.

"Oh, dear," cried Miss Minerva Halliday, and ran to her own compartment to plunge back and toss down a cascade of books.

"*Hamlet!*" she cried, "his father, yes? *A Christmas Carol. Four* ghosts! *Wuthering Heights.* Kathy *returns*, yes? To haunt the snows? Ah, *The Turn of the Screw,* and . . . *Rebecca!* Then—my favorite! *The Monkey's Paw!* Which?"

But the Orient ghost said not a Marley word. His eyes were locked, his mouth sewn with icicles.

"Wait!" she cried.

And opened the first book . . .

Where Hamlet stood on the castle wall and heard his ghost of a father moan, and so she said these words:

" 'Mark me . . . my hour is almost come . . . when I to sulphurous and tormenting flames . . . must render up myself . . .' "

And then she read:

" 'I am thy father's spirit, Doomed for a certain term to walk the night . . .' "

And again:

" '. . . if thou didst ever thy dear father love . . . O, God! . . . Revenge his foul and most unnatural murder . . .' "

And yet again:

" '. . . Murder most foul . . .' "

And the train ran in the night as she spoke the last words of Hamlet's father's ghost:

" '. . . Fare thee well at once . . .' "

" '. . . Adieu, adieu! Remember me.' "

And she repeated:

" '. . . remember me!' "

And the Orient ghost quivered. She seized a further book:

" '. . . Marley was dead, to begin with . . .' "

As the Orient train thundered across a twilight bridge above an unseen stream.

Her hands flew like birds.

" 'I am the Ghost of Christmas Past!' "

Then:

" 'The Phantom Rickshaw glided from the mist and clop-clopped off into the fog—' "

And wasn't there the faintest echo of a horse's hooves behind, within the Orient ghost's mouth?

" 'The beating beating beating, under the floor-boards, of the old man's Tell-tale Heart!' " she cried, softly.

And *there!* like the leap of a frog. The first pulse of the Orient ghost's heart in more than an hour.

The Germans down the corridor fired off a cannon of disbelief.

But *she* poured the medicine:

" 'The Hound bayed out on the Moor—' "

And the echo of that bay, that most forlorn cry, came from her traveling companion's soul, wailed from his throat.

As the night grew on and the moon arose and a Woman in White crossed a landscape, as the old nurse said and told, a bat that became a wolf that became a lizard scaled a wall on the ghastly passenger's brow.

And at last the train was silent with sleeping, and Miss Minerva Halliday let the last book drop with the thump of a body to the floor.

"*Requiescat in pace?*" whispered the Orient traveler, eyes shut.

"Yes." She smiled, nodding. "*Requiescat in pace.*" And they slept.

And at last they reached the sea.

And there was mist, which became fog, which became scatters of rain, like a proper drench of tears from a seamless sky.

Which made the ghastly passenger open, ungum his mouth, and murmur thanks for the haunted sky and the shore visited by phantoms of tide as the train slid into the shed where the mobbed exchange would be made, a full train becoming a full boat.

The Orient ghost stood well back, the last figure on a now self-haunted train.

"Wait," he cried, softly, piteously. "That boat! There's no place on it to hide! And the *customs*!"

But the customs men took one look at the pale face snowed under the dark cap and earmuffs, and swiftly flagged the wintry soul onto the ferry.

To be surrounded by dumb voices, ignorant elbows,

layers of people shoving as the boat shuddered and moved and the nurse saw her fragile icicle melt yet again.

It was a mob of children shrieking by that made her say: "Quickly!"

And she all but carried the wicker man in the wake of the boys and girls.

"No," cried the old passenger. "The noise!"

"It's special!" The nurse hustled him through a door. "A medicine! Here!"

The old man stared.

"Why," he murmured. "This is—a playroom."

She steered him into the midst of all the screams.

"Children! Storytelling time!"

They were about to run again when she added, "*Ghost*-story-telling time!"

She pointed casually to the ghastly passenger, whose pale moth fingers grasped the scarf about his icy throat.

"All fall *down*!" said the nurse.

The children plummeted with squeals all about the Orient traveler, like Indians around a teepee. They stared up along his body to where blizzards ran odd temperatures in his gaping mouth.

"You *do* believe in ghosts, *yes*?" she said.

"Oh, *yes*!" was the shout. "Yes!"

It was as if a ramrod had shot up his spine. The Orient traveler stiffened. The most brittle of tiny flinty

sparks fired his eyes. Winter roses budded in his cheeks. And the more the children leaned, the taller he grew, and the warmer his complexion. With one icicle finger he pointed at their faces.

"I," he whispered, "I," a pause. "Shall tell you a frightful tale. About a *real* ghost!"

"Oh, *yes!*" cried the children.

And he began to talk and as the fever of his tongue conjured fogs, lured mists, and invited rains, the children hugged and crowded close, a bed of charcoals on which he happily baked. And as he talked Nurse Halliday, backed off near the door, saw what he saw across the haunted sea, the ghost cliffs, the chalk cliffs, the safe cliffs of Dover and not so far beyond, waiting, the whispering towers, the murmuring castle deeps, where phantoms were as they had always been, with the still attics waiting. And staring, the old nurse felt her hand creep up her lapel toward her thermometer. She felt her own pulse. A brief darkness touched her eyes.

And then one child said: "Who *are* you?"

And gathering his gossamer shroud, the ghastly passenger whetted his imagination, and replied.

It was only the sound of the ferry landing whistle that cut short the long telling of midnight tales. And the parents poured in to seize their lost children, away from the Orient gentleman with the frozen eyes whose gently raving mouth shivered their marrows as he whispered and whispered until the ferry nudged the dock and the last boy was dragged, protesting, away, leaving the old man and his nurse alone in the children's playroom as the ferry stopped shuddering its delicious shudders, as if it had listened, heard, and deliriously enjoyed the long-before-dawn tales.

At the gangplank, the Orient traveler said, with a touch of briskness, "No. I'll need no help going down. Watch!"

And he strode down the plank. And even as the children had been tonic for his color, height, and vocal cords, so the closer he came to England, pacing, the firmer his stride, and when he actually touched the dock, a small happy burst of sound erupted from his thin lips and the nurse, behind him, stopped frowning, and let him run toward the train.

And seeing him dash like a child before her, she could only stand, riven with delight and something more than delight. And he ran and her heart ran with him and suddenly knew a stab of amazing pain, and a lid of darkness struck her and she swooned.

Hurrying, the ghastly passenger did not notice that the old nurse was not beside or behind him, so eagerly did he go.

At the train he gasped, "There!" safely grasping the

compartment handle. Only then did he sense a loss, and turned.

Minerva Halliday was not there.

And yet, an instant later, she arrived, looking paler than before, but with an incredibly radiant smile. She wavered and almost fell. This time it was he who reached out.

"Dear lady," he said, "you have been so kind."

"But," she said, quietly, looking at him, waiting for him to truly see her, "I am not leaving."

"You . . . ?"

"I am going with you," she said.

"But your plans?"

"Have changed. Now, I have nowhere *else* to go."

She half turned to look over her shoulder.

At the dock, a swiftly gathering crowd peered down at someone lying on the planks. Voices murmured and cried out. The word "doctor" was called several times.

The ghastly passenger looked at Minerva Halliday. Then he looked at the crowd and the object of the crowd's alarm lying on the dock: a medical thermometer lay broken under their feet. He looked back at Minerva Halliday, who still stared at the broken thermometer.

"Oh, my dear kind lady," he said, at last. "Come."

She looked into his face. "Larks?" she said.

He nodded. "Larks!"

And he helped her up into the train, which soon jolted and then dinned and whistled away along the tracks toward London and Edinburgh and moors and castles and dark nights and long years.

"I wonder who she was?" said the ghastly passenger, looking back at the crowd on the dock.

"Oh, Lord," said the old nurse. "I never really knew."

And the train was gone.

It took a full twenty seconds for the tracks to stop trembling.

CHAPTER 13

Nostrum Paracelsius Crook

"Don't tell me who I am. I don't want to know."

The words moved out into the silence of the great barn behind the incredibly huge House.

Nostrum Paracelsius Crook spoke them. He had been the first but three to arrive and now had threatened never to leave, which bent the backs and wrecked the souls of all who had gathered here the twilight of some days after the Homecoming.

Nostrum P. C., as he was known, had a crook in his back and a similar affliction halfway across his mouth. One eye, also, tended to be half shut or half open de-

pending on how you stared at him, and the eye behind the lid was pure fire crystal and tended to stay crossed.

"Or, in other words . . ." Nostrum P. C. paused and then said:

"Don't tell me what I am *doing*. I don't want to know."

There was a puzzled whisper amongst the members of the Family gathered in the lofty barn.

A third of their number had flown or scurried back across the sky or wolf-trotted along the riversides north and south and east and west, leaving at least sixty cousins, uncles, grandfathers, and strange visitors behind. Because—

"Why do I say all this?" Nostrum P. C. went on.

Yes, why? Five dozen or so strange faces leaned forward.

"The wars in Europe have ravened the sky, shredded the clouds, poisoned the winds. Even the west-to-east oceanic currents of the heavens are redolent of sulfur and brimstone. The trees of China, they say, from their recent wars, are bereft of birds. The Orient wise are thus grounded where the trees lie empty. Now, the same threatens in Europe. Our shadow cousins not long ago made it to the Channel and across to England where they might survive. But that is mere guesswork. When the last castles of England decay and the people waken from what they call superstition, our cousins may well be in failing health and soon be melted down to sod."

All gasped. There was a soft wail that stirred the Family.

"Most of you," the ancient man went on, "may stay on. You are welcome here. There are bins and cupolas and out-dwellings and peach trees aplenty, so settle in. It is however, an unhappy circumstance. Because of it I have said what I have said."

"Don't tell me what I am doing," Timothy recited.

"I don't want to know," whispered the five dozen Family members.

"But now," said Nostrum P. C., "we *must* know. *You* must know. Over the centuries we have given no name, found no label, that signified self, which summed up the totality of . . . us. Let us begin."

But before anyone could start there was a great silence at the front portal of the house, such a silence as might come from the repercussion of a thunderous knock never delivered. It was as if a vast mouth with wind-filled cheeks had exhaled upon the door and shivered it to announce all things half visible, there but not there.

The ghastly passenger had arrived with all the answers.

* * *

No one ever imagined or could figure how the ghastly passenger survived and made it across the world to October Country, upper Illinois. It was only guessed that perhaps somehow he prolonged himself in deserted abbeys and empty churches and lost graveyards of Scotland and England and finally sailed across in a ghost ship to land in Mystic Seaport, Connecticut, and somehow threaded his way among the forest, across the country, to finally arrive in upper Illinois.

This happened on a night when there was little rain except for a small patch of clouds that moved across the landscape and finally battered the front porch of the great House. There was a shimmering and stammering of locks on the portal and when the doors swung wide, there stood at long last the first of a fine new batch of immigrant members of the Family: the ghastly passenger with Minerva Halliday, looking remarkably dead for someone so dead.

Timothy's father, peering out at this half-perceived vibration of cold air, sensed an intelligence there that could respond to questions before they were asked. And so at last he said:

"Are you one of us?"

"Am I one *of* you, or *with* you?" the ghastly passenger replied. "And what are you, or we, or us? Can it be named? Is there a shape? What ambience is there? Are

we kin to autumn rains? Do we rise in mists from wet-
land moors? Do twilight fogs seem similar? Do we prowl
or run or lope? Are we shadows on a ruined wall? Are
we dusts shaken in sneezes from angel tombstones with
broken wings? Do we hover or fly or writhe in October
ectoplasms? Are we footsteps heard to waken us and
bump our skulls on nailed-shut lids? Are we batwing
heartbeats held in claw or hand or teeth? Do our cousins
weave and spell their lives like that creature lassoed to
the boy-child's neck?" He gestured.

Arach unraveled its spinneret in dark silence.

"Do we snug with *that*?" Again the gesture.

Mouse vanished in Timothy's vest.

"Do we move soundless? There?"

Anuba combed good Timothy's foot.

"Are we the mirror glimpses, unseen but there? Do
we abide in walls as mortuary beetles telling time? Is the
drafting breath upsucked in chimneys our terrible respiration? When clouds curdle the moon are we such
clouds? When rainspouts speak from the gargoyles'
mouths are we those tongueless sounds? Do we sleep by
day and swarm-glide the splendid night? When autumn
trees shower bullions are we that Midas stuff, a leaf-fall
that sounds the air in crisp syllables? What, what, oh
what are we? And who are you, and I, and all surround-
ing gasps of dead but undead cries? Ask not for whom

the funeral bell tolls. It tolls for thee and me and all the ghastly terribles who nameless wander in a Marley death of chains. Do I speak the truth?"

"Oh yes!" exclaimed Father. "Come in!"

"Yes!" cried Nostrum Paracelsius Crook.

"In," cried Timothy.

"In," pantomimed Anuba and Mouse and eight-legged Arach.

"In," whispered Timothy.

And the ghastly passenger lurched into the arms of his cousins to beg merciful lodgings for a thousand nights and a chorus of "ayes" soared up like a rain reversed and the door shut and the ghastly passenger and his wondrous nurse were home.

CHAPTER 14

The October People

All because of the cold exhalation of the ghastly passenger the inhabitants of the Autumn House suffered a delicious chill, shook down the ancient metaphors in their attic skulls and decided to gather at an even greater meeting of the October People.

Now that the Homecoming was over, certain terrible truths arrived. One moment the tree was empty of leaves in the autumn wind, and then, instantly, problems clustered upside down along the branches fanning wings and baring needle teeth.

The metaphor was extreme, but the Autumn council was serious. The Family must at last decide as the ghastly cousin suggested, who and what it was. Dark strangers must be indexed and filed.

Who, amongst the invisible mirror images, was oldest?

"I," came the attic whisper. "I," A Thousand Times Great Grandmère whistled her toothless gums. "There is no other."

"Said and done," agreed Thomas the Tall.

"Agreed," said the mouse-dwarf at the shadowed end of the long council table, his hands freckled with Egyptian spots pressing the mahogany surface.

The table thumped. Something beneath the table lid gave a laughing bump. No one looked to see.

"How many of us are table knockers, how many walkers, shamblers, lopers? How many take the sun, how many shadow the moon?"

"Not so fast," said Timothy, whose task it was to scribble the facts, plain breadfruit or otherwise.

"How many branches of the Family are death-related?"

"We," said other attic voices, the wind that crept through the cracked timbers and whined the roof. "We are the October People, the autumn folk. That is the truth in an almond husk, a nightweed shell."

"Far too nebulous," said Thomas the Short, not like his name, Tall.

"Let us go around the table of travelers, those who

have walked, run, spidered, strode in time as well as space, on air as well as turf. I think we are in the Twenty-one Presences, an occult summing of the various tributaries of leaves blown off far ten thousand mile trees to settle in harvests here."

"Why all this frittering and fuss?" said the next-oldest gentleman half down the table, he who had raised onions and baked bread for the pharaoh's tombs. "Everyone knows what each of us does. I fire the rye loaves and bundle the green onions that bouquet the clasped embrace of Nile Valley kings. I provender banquets in Death's hall where a baker's dozen of pharaohs are seated on gold and whose breath is yeast and green rushes, whose exhalation is eternal life. What else must you know of me, or any other?"

"Your data is sufficient." The Tall One nodded. "But we need a moonless night résumé from all. With this knowledge we can stand together when this mindless war reaches its peak!"

"War?" Timothy glanced up. "What war?" And then clapped his palm over his mouth and blushed. "Sorry."

"No need, boy." The father of all darkness spoke. "Listen, now, let me provide the history of the rising tide of disbelief. The Judeo-Christian world is a devastation. The burning bush of Moses will not fire. Christ, from the tomb, fears to come forth should he be unrecognized by doubting Thomas. The shadow of Allah melts at noon. So Christians and Muslims confront a world torn by many wars to finalize yet a larger. Moses did not walk down the mountain for he never walked up. Christ did not die for he was never born. All this, all this mind you, is of great importance to us, for we are the reverse side of the coin tossed in the air to fall heads or tails. Does the unholy or holy win? Ah, but look: the answer is neither none or *what*? Not only is Jesus lonely and Nazareth in ruins, but the populace at large believes in Nothing. There is no room for either glorious or terrible. We are in danger, too, trapped in the tomb with an uncrucified carpenter, blown away with the burning bush as the east's Black Cubicle cracks its mortar and falls. The world is at war. They do not name us the Enemy, no, for that would give us flesh and substance. You must see the face or the mask in order to strike through one to deface the other. They war against us by pretending, no, assuring each other we have no flesh and substance. It is a figment war. And if we believe as these disbelievers believe, we will flake our bones to litter the winds."

Ah, whispered the many shadows at the council. *Eeee,* came the murmur. *No.*

"But yes," said Father in his ancient shroud. "Once the war was simply between Christians and Muslims and ourselves. As long as they believed in their sermoned lives, and disbelieved in us, we had more than a mythical flesh. We had something to fight for to survive. But now that the world is filled with warriors who do not attack, but simply turn away or walk through us, who do not even argue us as half unreal, we find ourselves weaponless. One more tidal wave of neglect, one more titanic rainfall of nothings from nowhere and the Apocalypse, arriving, will with one neglectful gust blow out our candles. A dust storm of sorts will sneeze across the world and our Family will be no more. Destroyed by a single phrase which, if listened to and leaned on, simply says: you *do* not exist, you *did* not exist, you never *were*."

"Ah. No. Eeee. No, no," came the whisper.

"Not so fast," said Timothy in full scribble.

"What is the plan of attack?"

"Beg pardon?"

"Well," said the dark unseen adopted mother to Timothy the Seen, Timothy the well lit, the plainly found, "you have drawn up the fierce outlines of Armageddon. You have all but destroyed us with words. Now raise us up so we are half October People and half Lazarus cousins. We know whom we fight. Now how do we win? The counterattack, if you please."

"That's better," said Timothy, tongue between his teeth, writing slowly to his mother's slower pronunciations.

"The problem is," interjected the ghastly passenger, "we must make people believe in us only *up to a point*! If they believe in us too much they will forge hammers and sharpen stakes, manufacture crucifixes and forge mirrors. Damned if we do, damned if we don't. How do we fight without appearing to fight? How do we manifest without making our focus too clear? Tell people we are not dead and yet have been duly buried?"

The dark father brooded.

"Spread out," someone said.

Those at the table turned as one to stare at the mouth from which this suggestion had fallen. Timothy's. He glanced up, realizing that, not intending to, he had spoken.

"Again?" commanded his father.

"Spread out," said Timothy, eyes shut.

"Go on, child."

"Well," said Timothy, "look at us, all in one room. Look at us, all in one House. Look at us, all in one town!"

Timothy's mouth fell shut.

"Well," said the shrouded parent.

Timothy squeaked like a mouse, which brought Mouse from his lapel. The arachnid on his neck trembled. Anuba stoked up a roar.

"Well," said Timothy, "we've only got so much room in the House for all the leaves that fall out of the sky, for all the animals that move through the woods, for all the bats that fly, all the clouds that come to drop rain. We have only a few towers left, one of which is now occupied by the ghastly passenger and his nurse. That tower is taken and we only have so many wine bins left in which to stash old wine, we only have so many closets in which to hang gossamer ectoplasms, we only have so much wall room for new mice, we only have so many corners for cobwebs. That being so, we must find a way to distribute the souls, to move people out of the House and away to some safe places around the country."

"And how do we do that?"

"Well," said Timothy, feeling everyone gazing at him, for after all he was only a child advising all these ancient people on how they should live—or how they should go out and be undead, was more like it.

"Well," continued Timothy, "we have someone who could make distribution. She can search the country for souls, look for empty bodies and empty lives and when she finds great canisters that are not full, and little tiny glasses that are half empty, she can take these bodies and empty these souls and make room for those of us who want to travel."

"And who is this other person?" said someone, knowing the answer.

"The person who can help us distribute souls is in the attic now. She sleeps and dreams, dreams and sleeps, in far places, and I think if we go ask her to help our search she will. In the meantime let us think on her and become familiar with the way that she lives, the way that she travels."

"And who is this, again?" said a voice.

"Her name?" said Timothy. "Why, Cecy."

"Yes," said a fine and lovely voice that troubled the council air.

Her attic voice spoke.

"I will be," said Cecy, "like someone who sows the winds to put down a seed of a flower at some future time. Let me gather one soul at a time and move across the land and find a proper place to put it down. Some miles from here, far beyond the town, there's an empty farm that was abandoned some years ago during a storm of dust. Let there be a volunteer from among all our strange relatives. Who will step forward and allow me to travel to that far place and that empty farm to take over and raise children and exist beyond the threat of the cities? Who shall it be?"

"Why," said a voice from the midst of great beatings

of wings at the far end of the table, "should it not be me?" said Uncle Einar. "I have the capacity of flight and can make it partly there if you assist me, take hold of my soul, seize on my mind, and help me to travel."

"Yes, Uncle Einar," said Cecy. "Indeed you, the winged one, are proper. Are you ready?"

"Yes," said Uncle Einar.

"Well then," said Cecy, "let us begin."

CHAPTER 15

Uncle Einar

"It will take only a minute," said Uncle Einar's good wife.

"I refuse," he said. "And that takes me one *second*."

"I've worked all morning," she said. "And you refuse to help? It's about to rain."

"Let it rain," he cried. "I'll not be struck by lightning just to air your clothes."

"But you're so *quick* at it," she said.

"Again, I refuse." His vast tarpaulin wings hummed nervously behind his back.

She gave him a slender rope on which were tied two dozen fresh-washed clothes. He turned it in his fingers with distaste in his eyes. "So it's come to this," he muttered, bitterly. "To this, to this, to this."

After all the days and weeks of Cecy searching the winds and seeing the land and finding the farms that were not quite right, she at last had found an empty farm, with the people gone and the house deserted. Cecy sent him here on a long transit to search for a possible wife and refuge from a disbelieving world, and here he was, stranded.

"Don't cry; you'll wet the clothes down again," she said. "Jump now, run them up and it'll be finished in a jiffy."

"Run them up," he said in mockery, both hollow and terribly wounded. "Let it thunder, let it pour!"

"If it was a nice sunny day I wouldn't ask," she said. "All my washing gone for nothing. They'll hang about the house—"

That *did* it. If it was anything he hated it was clothes flagged and festooned so a man had to creep under them on the way across a room. He boomed his vast wings.

"But only as far as the pasture fence," he said.

"Only!" she cried.

Whirl . . . and up he jumped, his wings cleaving and loving the cool air, to roar low across the farmland, trailing the line of clothes in a vast fluttering loop, drying them in the pounding concussion and backwash from his wings.

"Catch!"

A minute later, returned, he sailed the clothes, dry as fresh wheat, down on a series of clean blankets she'd laid out.

"Much thanks!" she cried.

"Gahh!" he shouted, and flew off to brood under the sour-apple tree.

Uncle Einar's beautiful silklike wings hung like sea-green sails behind him and whirred and whispered from his shoulders when he sneezed or turned around swiftly.

Did he hate his wings? Far from it. In his youth he'd always flown nights. Nights were the times for winged men. Daylight held dangers, always had, always would, but night, ah, night, he had sailed over far lands and farther seas. With no danger to himself. It had been a rich, full flying and an exhilaration.

But now he could not fly at night.

On his way here to this damnable, luckless farm he had drunk too much rich crimson wine. "I'll be all right," he had told himself, blearily, as he beat his long way under the morning stars, over the moon-dreaming country hills. And then—crack out of the sky—

God's or the Universe's bolt of blue lightning! A high tension tower, invisible till the last second against the dark bowl of night.

Like a netted duck! A great sizzling! His face was blown black by blazed St. Elmo's fires. He fended off the fire with a terrific back-jumping percussion of his wings, and fell.

His hitting the moonlit meadow made a noise like a huge telephone book dropped from the sky.

Early the next morning, his dew-sodden wings shaking violently, he arose. It was still dark. There was a faint bandage of dawn stretched across the east. Soon the bandage would stain and all flight would be restricted. There was nothing to do but take refuge in the forest and wait out the day in the deepest thicket until another night gave his wings a hidden movement in the sky.

In this fashion his future wife found him.

During the day, which was warm, young Brunilla Wexley was out to udder a lost cow, for she carried a silver pail in one hand as she sidled through thickets and pleaded cleverly to the unseen cow to please return home or burst her gut with unplucked milk. The fact that the cow would have most certainly come home when her teats really needed pulling did not concern Brunilla Wexley. It was a sweet excuse for forest-journeying, thistle-blowing, and dandelion-chewing all of which Brunilla was doing when she stumbled upon Uncle Einar.

Asleep near a bush, he seemed a man under a green shelter.

"Oh," said Brunilla, with a fever. "A man. In a camp-tent."

Uncle Einar awoke. The camp-tent spread like a large green fan behind him.

"Oh," said Brunilla, the cow-searcher. "A man with wings. Yes, yes, at last. Cecy said she would send you! It's Einar, yes?!"

It was a fancy thing to see a winged man and she was proud to meet him. She began to talk to him and in an hour they were old friends, and in two hours she'd quite forgotten his wings were there.

"You look banged around," she said. "That right wing looks very bad. You'd best let me fix it. You won't be able to fly on it, anyway. Did Cecy tell you I live alone with my children? I'm an astrologer of sorts, most peculiar, strange, almost psychic. And, as you see, quite ugly."

He insisted she was not, and he didn't mind the psychic. But wasn't she afraid of him? he asked.

"Jealous would be more near it," she said. "*May* I?" And she stroked his large, green, membraned veils with careful envy. He shuddered at the touch and put his tongue between his teeth.

So there was nothing for it but that he come to her house and have an ointment on that bruise, and my! what a burn across his face, beneath his eyes.

"Lucky you weren't blinded," she said. "How'd it happen?"

"I dared the heavens!" he said, and they were at her farm, hardly noticing they'd walked a mile, watchful of each other.

Well, a day passed, and another. The day came that he thanked her at her door and said he must be going. After all, Cecy wanted him to meet a number of other possible ladies in the far country before he decided where to tarpaulin-fold his wings and settle in.

It was twilight, and he must travel many miles to a farm farther on.

"Thank you, and goodbye," he said, as he unfurled his wings and started to fly off in the dusk . . . and crashed straight on into a maple tree.

"Oh!" she cried, and ran to stand over his unconscious body.

That *did* it. When he woke the next hour he knew he'd fly no nights ever again. His delicate night-perception was gone. The winged telepathy that told him where towers, trees, and wires stood across his path; the fine, clear vision and mentality that guided him 'twixt cliff, pole, and pine—all of it was gone. And Cecy's distant voice, no help. That crack across his face, the blue electrical flames, had sloughed off his perceptions, perhaps forever.

"How'm I to fly back to Europe?" he groaned, pitifully. "If I want someday to fly there!"

"Oh," Brunilla Wexley said, studying the floor. "Who wants Europe?"

And so they were married. The ceremony was brief, if a little inverted and dark and mildly different to Brunilla, but it ended well. Uncle Einar stood with his fresh bride thinking that he didn't dare fly back to Europe in the daytime, which was the only time he could safely see now, for fear of being seen and shot; but it didn't matter any more, for with Brunilla beside him, Europe had less and less fascination for him.

He didn't have to see very well to fly straight up, or come down. So it was only natural that on their wedding night he gathered Brunilla and soared straight up in the clouds.

A farmer, five miles over, glanced at the sky about midnight and saw faint glows and crackles.

"Heat lightnin'," he figured.

They didn't come back down until dawn with the dew.

* * *

The marriage took. She was so wing-proud of him, it lifted her to think she was the only woman in the world married to a winged man. "Who else could say it?" she asked her mirror. And the answer was: "No one!"

He, on the other hand, found great beauty behind her face, great kindness and understanding. He made some changes in his diet to fit her thinking, and was careful that his wings did not knock porcelains and spill lamps. He also changed his sleeping habits, since he couldn't fly nights anyhow. And she in turn fixed chairs so they were comfortable for his wings and said things he loved to hear. "We're all in cocoons," she said. "I'm plain bread. But one day I'll break out wings as fine and handsome as yours!"

"You broke out long ago," he said.

"Yes," she had to admit. "I know just which day it was. In the woods when I looked for a cow and found a camp-tent!" And they laughed, and in that moment a hidden beauty slipped her from her homeliness, like a sword from its case.

As for her fatherless children, three boys and a girl, who, for their energy, seemed to have wings, they popped up like toadstools on hot summer days to ask Uncle Einar to sit under the apple tree and fan them with his cooling wings and tell them wild starlit tales of youth and sky excursions. So he told them of the winds and cloud textures, and what a star feels like melting in your mouth, and the taste of high mountain air, and how it feels to be a pebble dropped from Mt. Everest, turning to a green bloom, flowering your wings just before striking the ageless snow!

This was his marriage, then.

And today, here sat Uncle Einar, fustering under the tree, grown impatient and unkind; not because this was his desire, but because after the long wait, his night-flight sense had never returned. Here he sat despondently, resembling a green summer sun-parasol, abandoned for the season by reckless vacationers who once sought refuge under its spread shadow. Was he to sit here forever, afraid to fly, save as a clothes-drier for his good wife, or a fanner of children on hot August noons? Ye gods! Think!

His one occupation, flight, running family errands, quicker than storms, faster than telegraphs. Like a boomerang he'd whickled over hills and valleys and like a thistle landed.

But now? Bitterness! His wings quivered behind him.

"Papa, fan us," said his small daughter.

The children stood before him, looking up at his dark face.

"No," he said.

"Fan us, Papa," said the honorable new son.

"It's a cool day, there'll soon be rain," said Uncle Einar.

"There's a wind blowing, Papa. The wind'll blow the clouds way," said the second, very small son.

"Will you come watch us, Papa?"

"Run on, run on," Einar told them. "Let Papa brood."

Again he thought of old skies, night skies, cloudy skies, all kinds of skies. Was it to be his fate to scull pastures in fear of being seen breaking wing on the silo, or cracking up on a kindling fence? Gah!

"Come watch us, Papa," said the girl.

"We're goin' to the hill," said one boy. "With all the kids from town."

Uncle Einar chewed his knuckles. "What hill's that?"

"The Kite Hill, of course!" they sang together.

Now he examined the three.

They each held large paper kites against their gasping bosoms, their faces bathed with anticipation and animal glowing. In their small fingers were balls of white twine. From the kites, colored red, blue, yellow, and green, hung appendages of cotton and silk strips.

"We'll fly our kites! Come see!"

"No," he said. "I'd be *seen*!"

"You could hide and watch from the woods. We want you to see."

153

"The kites?" he said.

"Made 'em ourselves. Just because we know how."

"How do you know how?"

"You're our papa!" was the instant cry. "*That's* how!"

He looked from one to the second to the third. "A kite festival, is it?"

"Yes, sir!"

"I'm going to win," said the girl.

"No, *me*!" the boys contradicted. "Me, me!"

"God!" roared Uncle Einar. He leaped up with a deafening kettledrum of wings. "Children! Children, I love you, I love you!"

"What? What's wrong?" The children backed off.

"Nothing!" chanted Einar, flexing his wings to their greatest propulsion and plundering. Whoom! they whammed together like cymbals and the children fell flat in the backwash! "I have it, I *have* it! I'm free again, free! Fire in the flue! Feather on the wind! Brunilla!" He called to the house. She stuck her head out. "I'm free!" he cried, flushed and tall. "Listen! I don't need the night! I can fly by day, now! I don't need the night! I'll fly *every* day and *any* day of the year from now on, and nobody'll know, and nobody'll shoot me down, and, and—but, God, I waste time! Look!"

And as the shocked members of his family watched he seized the cotton tail from one of the kites, tied it to his belt, grabbed the twine ball and gripped one end between his teeth, gave the other end to his children, and up, up into the air he flew, away into the wind!

And across the meadows and over the farms his daughter and sons ran, feeding out string into the daylit sky, shrieking and stumbling, and Brunilla stood out on the farm porch and waved and laughed to know that from now on her family would run and fly in joy.

The children pell-melled to the far Kite Hill and stood, the three of them, holding the ball of twine in their eager, proud fingers, each tugging, directing, pulling.

The children from town came running with *their* small kites to let up on the wind, and they saw the great green kite dipping and hovering in the sky and they exclaimed:

"Oh, oh, what a kite! Oh, oh! I wish I had a kite like that! Oh, what a kite! Where'd you get it!?"

"Our father made it!" cried the honorable daughter and the two fine sons, and gave an exultant pull on the twine and the humming, thundering kite in the sky flew and soared and wrote a great and magical exclamation mark across a cloud!

CHAPTER 16

The Whisperers

The list was long, the need was manifest.

Manifestations of need took many shapes and forms. Some were solid flesh, some were evanescent ambiences which grew on the air, some partook of the clouds, some the wind, some merely the night, but all needed a place to hide, a place to be stashed, whether in wine cellars or attics or formed in stone statues on the marble porch of the House. And among these were mere whispers. You had to listen closely to hear the needs.

And the whispers said:

"Lie low. Be still. Speak and rise not. Give no ear to the cannons' cries and shouts. For what they shout is

doom and death—with no ghosts manifest and spirits given heart. They say not yes to us, the grand army of the fearsome resurrected, but no, the terrible no, which makes the bat drop wingless and the wolf lie crippled and all coffins riven with ice and nailed with Eternity's frost from which no Family breath can suspire to roam the weather in vapors and mist.

"Stay, oh, stay in the great House, sleep with telltale hearts which drum the timbered floor. Stay, oh, stay, all silence be. Hide. Wait. Wait."

CHAPTER 17

The Theban Voice

"I was the bastard child of the hinges at the great wall of Thebes," it said. "By what do I mean bastard or, for that matter, hinges? A vast door in a wall at Thebes, yes?"

All at the table nodded, impatiently. *Yes.*

"Quickly then," said the mist within a vapor inside the merest sneeze of shadow, "when the wall was built and the double gate chiseled from vast timbers, the first hinge in the world was invented on which to hang the gates so they could be opened with ease. And they were opened often to let the worshippers in to worship Isis or Osirus or Bubastis or Ra. But the high priests had not as yet magicked themselves into tricks, had not as yet sensed that the gods must have voices, or at least incense so that as the smoke arose one could configure the spirals and whiffs and read symbols or air and space. The incense came later. They did not know, but voices were needed. I was that voice."

"Ah?" the Family leaned forward. "So?"

"They had invented the hinge made of solid bronze, an eternity of metal, but had not invented the lubricant to make the hinge gape quietly. So when the great Theban doors were opened, I was born. Very small at first, my voice, a squeak, a squeal, but soon, the vibrant declaration of the gods. Hidden, a secret declaration, unseen, Ra and Bubastis spoke through me. The holy worshippers, riven, now paid as much attention to my syllables, my perambulating squeals and grindings as they did to the golden masks and harvest-blanching fists!"

"I never thought of that." Timothy looked up in gentle surprise.

"Think," said the voice from the Theban hinges three thousand years lost in time.

"Continue," said all.

"And seeing," said the voice, "that the worshippers tilted their heads to catch my pronunciamentos, garbed in mystery and waiting for interpretation, instead of oil-ing the bronze hasps, a lector was appointed, a high priest who translated my merest creak and murmur as a hint from Osiris, an inclination from Bubastis, an approbation from the Sun Himself."

The presence paused and gave several examples of the creak and slur of the hinge binding itself. This was music.

"Once born, I never died. Almost but no. While oils glistened the gates and doors of the world, there was always one door, one hinge, where I lodged for a night, a year, or a mortal lifetime. So I have made it across continents, with my own linguistics, my own treasures of knowledge, and rest here among you, representative of all the openings and closures of a vast world. Put not butter, nor grease, nor bacon-rind upon my resting places."

A gentle laughter, in which all joined.

"How shall we write you down?" asked Timothy.

"As a tribesman of the Talkers with no wind, no need of air. The self-sufficient speakers of the night at noon."

"Say that again."

"The small voice that asks of the dead who arrive for admission at the gate of paradise: 'In your life, did you know enthusiasm?' If the answer is yes you enter the sky. If no, you fall to burn in the pit."

"The more questions I ask, the longer your answers get."

" 'The Theban Voice.' Write that."

Timothy wrote.

"How do you spell 'Theban'?" he said.

CHAPTER 18

Make Haste to Live

Mademoiselle Angelina Marguerite was perhaps strange, to some grotesque, to many a nightmare, but most certainly a puzzle of inverted life.

Timothy did not know that she even existed until many months after that grand, happily remembered Homecoming.

For she lived, or existed, or in the final analysis *hid* in the shadowed acreage behind the great tree where stood markers with names and dates peculiar to the Family. Dates from when the Spanish Armada broke on the Irish coast and its women, to birth boys with dark, and girls with darker, hair. The names recalled the glad

OLIVE: GOLDSM
N. OE: 15. APR.
1774.
Æ. 45 YEAR.

times of the Inquisition or the Crusades—children who rode happily into Muslim graves. Some stones, larger than others, celebrated the suffering of witches in a Massachusetts town. All of the markers had sunk in place as the House took boarders from other centuries. What lay beneath the stones was known only to a small rodent and a smaller arachnid.

But it was the name Angelina Marguerite that took Timothy's breath. It spelled softly on the tongue. It was a relish of beauty.

"How long ago did she die?" Timothy asked.

"Ask rather," said Father, "how soon will she be *born*."

"But she *was* born a long time ago," said Timothy. "I can't make out the date. Surely—"

"Surely," said the tall, gaunt, pale man at the head of the dinner table, who got taller and gaunter and paler by the hour, "surely if I can trust my ears and ganglion, she will be *truly* born in a fortnight."

"How *much* is a fortnight?" asked Timothy.

Father sighed. "Look it up. She will not stay beneath her stone."

"You mean—?"

"Stand watch. When the grave marker trembles and the ground stirs, you will at last see Angelina Marguerite."

"Will she be as beautiful as her name?"

"Gods, yes. I would hate to wait while an old crone got younger and younger, taking years to melt her back to beauty. If we are fortunate, she'll be a Castilian rose. Angelina Marguerite waits. Go see if she's awake. *Now!*"

Timothy ran, one tiny friend on his cheek, another in his blouse, a third following.

"Oh, Arach, Mouse, Anuba," he said, hurrying through the old dark House, "what does Father *mean*?"

"Quiet." The eight legs rustled in his ear.

"Listen," said an echo from his blouse.

"Stand aside," said the cat. "Let me lead!"

And arriving at the grave with the pale stone, as smooth as a maiden's cheek, Timothy knelt and put that ear with its invisible weaver against the cool marble, so both might hear.

Timothy shut his eyes.

At first: stone silence.

And again, nothing.

He was about to leap up in confusion when the tickling in his ear said: *Wait.*

And deep under he heard what he thought was the single beat of a buried heart.

The soil under his knees pulsed three times swiftly.

Timothy fell back.

"Father told the truth!"

"Yes," said the whisper in his ear. "Yes," echoed the fur-ball thing in his blouse.

Anuba purred.

Yes!

He did not return to the pale gravestone, for it was so terrible and mysterious that he cried, not knowing why.

"Oh, that poor lady."

"Not poor, my dear," said his mother.

"But she's *dead*!"

"But not for long. Patience."

Still he could not visit, but sent his messengers to listen and come back.

The heartbeats increased. The ground shook with nervous tremors. A tapestry wove itself in his ear. His blouse pocket squirmed. Anuba ran in circles.

The time is near.

And then half through a long night with a storm freshly departed, a lightning bolt stabbed the graveyard to invigorate a celebration—

And Angelina Marguerite was born.

At three in the morning, the soul's midnight, Timothy looked out his window to see a procession of candles lighting the path to the tree and that one special stone.

Glancing up, candelabra in hand, Father gestured. Panicked or not, Timothy must attend.

He arrived to find the Family around the grave, their candles burning.

Father handed Timothy a small implement.

"Some spades bury, some reveal. Be the first to shovel earth."

Timothy dropped the spade.

"Pick it up," said Father. "Move!"

Timothy stuck the spade into the mound. A trip-hammering of heartbeat sounded. The gravestone cracked.

"Good!" And Father dug. The others followed until at last the most beautiful golden case he had ever seen, with a Royal Castilian insignia on its lid, came into sight, to be laid out under the tree to much laughter.

"How can they *laugh*?" cried Timothy.

"Dear child," said his mother. "It is a triumph over death. Everything turned upside down. She is not buried, but *unburied,* a grand reason for joy. Fetch wine!"

He brought two bottles to be poured in a dozen glasses that were lifted as a dozen voices murmured, "Oh, come forth, Angelina Marguerite, as a maiden, girl, baby, and thence to the womb and the eternity before Time!"

Then the box was opened.

And beneath the bright lid was a layer of—

"Onions?!" Timothy exclaimed.

And indeed, like a freshet of grass from the Nile banks, the onions were there, spring-green and lush and savory on the air.

And beneath the onions—

"Bread!" said Timothy.

Sixteen small loaves baked within the hour, with golden crusts like the lip of the box, and a smell of yeast and the warm oven that was the box.

"Bread and onions," said the oldest near-uncle in his Egyptian cerements, leaning to point into the garden box. "I planted these onions and bread. For the long journey not down the Nile to oblivion but up the Nile to the source, the Family, and then the time of the seed, the pomegranate with a thousand buds, one ripe each month, surrounded by encirclements of life, millions crying to be born. And *so* . . . ?"

"Bread and onions." Timothy joined the smiles. "Onions and bread!"

The onions had been put aside with the bread sheaved near them to reveal a gossamer veil laid over the face in the box.

Mother gestured. "Timothy?"

Timothy fell back.

"No!"

"She's not afraid to be *seen*. You must not be afraid to *see*. Now."

He took hold and pulled.

The veil plumed on the air like a puff of white smoke and blew away.

And Angelina Marguerite lay there with her face up-turned to the candlelight, her eyes shut, her mouth en-closing the faintest smile.

And she was a joy and a delight and a lovely toy crated and shipped from another time.

The candlelight trembled at the sight. The Family knew an earthquake of response. Their exclamations flooded the dark air. Not knowing what to do, they ap-plauded the golden hair, the fine high cheekbones, the arched eyebrows, the small and perfect ears, the satisfied but not self-satisfied mouth, fresh from a thousand years' sleep, her bosom a slender hillock, her hands like ivory pendants, the feet tiny and asking to be kissed, there seemed no need for shoes. Good Lord, they would *carry* her *anywhere*!

Anywhere! thought Timothy.

"I don't understand," he said. "How can this *be*?"

"This *is*," someone whispered.

And the whisper had come from the breathing mouth of this creature come alive.

"But—" said Timothy.

"Death is mysterious." Mother brushed Timothy's cheek. "Life even more so. Choose. And whether you blow away in dust at life's end or arrive at youngness and go back to birth and within birth, that is *stranger* than strange, yes?"

"Yes, but—"

"Accept." Father lifted his wineglass. "Celebrate this miracle."

And Timothy indeed saw the miracle, this daughter of time, with a face of youngness which became younger, yes, and even younger as he stared. It was as if she lay beneath a smoothly flowing, slowly passing stream of clear water which washed her cheeks with shadows and light and trembled her eyelids and purified her flesh.

Angelina Marguerite at this moment opened her eyes. They were the soft blue of the delicate veins in her temples.

"Well," she whispered. "Is this birth, or rebirth?"

Quiet laughter from all.

"One or the other. Other or none." Timothy's mother reached out. "Welcome. Stay. Soon enough you will leave for your sublime destiny."

"But," Timothy protested yet again.

"Never doubt. Simply *be*."

An hour younger than a minute ago, Angelina Marguerite took Mother's hand.

"Is there a cake with candles? Is this my first birthday or my nine hundred and ninety-*ninth*?"

Seeking the answer, more wine was poured.

Sunsets are loved because they vanish.

Flowers are loved because they go.

The dogs of the field and the cats of the kitchen are loved because soon they must depart.

These are not the sole reasons, but at the heart of morning welcomes and afternoon laughters is the promise of farewell. In the gray muzzle of an old dog we see goodbye. In the tired face of an old friend we read long journeys beyond returns.

So it was with Angelina Marguerite and the Family, but most of all with Timothy.

Make haste to live was the motto embroidered on a great hall carpet over which they walked or ran each minute of each hour of the day that the lovely maid occupied their lives. For she was diminishing from nineteen to eighteen-and-one-half to eighteen-and-one-quarter, even as they stared and put out their hands to quell this endless yet beautiful retrogression.

"Wait for me!" Timothy cried one day, seeing her face

and body melt from beauty to beauty, like a candle lit and never ceasing.

"Catch me if you can!" And Angelina Marguerite ran down across a meadow with Timothy weeping in pursuit.

Exhausted, with a great laugh, she fell and waited for him to drop near.

"Caught," he cried. "Trapped!"

"No," she said, gently, and took his hand. "Never, dear cousin. Listen."

Then she explained:

"I shall be this, eighteen, for a little while, and then seventeen and sixteen a small while, and oh, Timothy, while I am this and then that age, I must find me a quick love, a swift romance, in the town below, and not let them know I come down from this hill or this House, and release myself to joy for a little while before I am fifteen and fourteen and thirteen and then the innocence of twelve before the pulses start and the blood manifests, and then eleven and ignorant but happy, and ten—even happier. And then again, Timothy, if only somewhere along the way backward, you and I could conjoin, clasp hands in friendship, clasp bodies in joy, how fine, yes?"

"I don't know what you're *talking* about!"

"How old are you, Timothy?"

"Ten, I guess."

"Ah, yes. So you *don't* know what I say."

She leaned forward suddenly and gave him such a kiss on his mouth that his eardrums fractured and the soft spot on his skull ached.

"Does that give you a small idea of what you'll miss by not loving me?" she said.

Timothy blushed all over. His soul leaped out from his body and rushed back in in a storm.

"Almost," he whispered.

"Eventually," she said, "I must leave."

"That's terrible," he cried. "Why?"

"I must, dear cousin, for if I stay too long in any one place they will notice, as the months pass, that in October I was eighteen, and in November seventeen and then sixteen, and by Christmas ten, and with spring two, and then one, and then search and seek to find some flesh to mother me as I hide back in her womb to visit that Forever from whence we all came to visit Time and vanish in Eternity. So Shakespeare said."

"*Did* he?"

"Life is a visit, rounded by sleeps. I, being different, came from the sleep of Death. I run to hide in the sleep of Life. Next spring I will be a seed stored in the honeycomb of some maiden/wife, eager for collisions, ripe for life."

"You *are* strange," said Timothy.

"Very."

"Have there been many like you since the world began?"

"Few that we know. But aren't I fortunate, to be born from the grave, then buried in some child bride's pomegranate maze?"

"No *wonder* they were celebrating. All that laughter!" said Timothy, "and the *wine*!"

"No wonder," said Angelina Marguerite, and leaned for another kiss.

"Wait!"

Too late. Her mouth touched his. A furious blush fired his ears, burnt his neck, broke and rebuilt his legs, banged his heart and rose to crimson his entire face. A vast motor started in his loins and died nameless.

"Oh, Timothy," she said, "what a shame that we could not truly meet, you moving on to your grave, and I to a sweet oblivion of flesh and procreation."

"Yes," said Timothy, "a shame."

"Do you know what goodbye means? It means God be with you. Goodbye, Timothy."

"What?!"

"Goodbye!"

And before he could stagger to his feet she had fled up in the House to vanish forever.

* * *

Some said that she was seen later in the village, almost seventeen, and the week after that in a town across country, reaching and then leaving sixteen, then in Boston. The sum? Fifteen! And later on a ship bound for France, a girl of twelve.

From there her history fell into mist. Soon a letter arrived that described a child of five who stayed some few days in Provence. A traveler from Marseilles said a two-year-old, passing in a woman's arms, crowed and laughed some inarticulate message about some country, some town, a tree, and a House. But that, others said, was bumbershoot and poppycock.

The sum that set the seal on Angelina Marguerite was an Italian count passing through Illinois who, savoring the victuals and vintages at a mid-state hostel, told of a remarkable encounter with a Roman countess, pregnant and full ripe with child, whose eye had the eye of Angelina and the mouth of Marguerite and the shining of the soul of both. But, again, nonsense!

Ashes to ashes, dust to dust?

Timothy, at dinner one night surrounded by his Family, and napkinning his tears, said:

"Angelina means like an angel, yes? And Marguerite is a flower?"

"Yes," someone said.

"Well then," murmured Timothy. "Flowers and angels. Not ashes to ashes. Dust to dust. Angels and flowers."

"Let's drink to that," said all.

And they did.

CHAPTER 19

The Chimney Sweeps

But they were more than that.

They hollowed, they lingered, they roared down and wafted up, but they did not actually sweep the chimney vents and flues.

They occupied them. They came from far places to live there. And whether they were ethereal, sussurance of spirit, reminiscence of ghost, ambience of light, shadow, and slept or wakened soul, none could say.

They traveled in clouds, the high cirrus clouds of summer, and fell in thunderous frights of lightning when storms prevailed. Or often without benefit of cirrus or alto stratus they came upon the open sky meadows and

could be seen brushing the acres of wheat or lifting the veils of falling snow as if to peer at their final destination: the House and the ninety-nine or some said one hundred chimneys.

Ninety-nine or one hundred chimneys, which gasped at the skies asking to be filled, to be fed, and this hollow utterance pulled from the atmosphere each passing breeze, each moving weather, from all directions.

So the shapeless and invisible winds arrived one by one, carrying the semblance of their old weathers with them. And if they had names at all it was monsoon or sirocco or santana. And the ninety-nine or one hundred chimneys let them sift, wander, fall to lodge their summer solstice tempers and wintry blasts in the sooted bricks there to resummon themselves on August noons as crooning breeze or sound late nights with sounds like dying souls or then again reverberant of that melancholy suffering of sound, the foghorn, far out on the peninsulas of life, stranded on shipwreck crags, a thousand funerals in one, a lament of burial seas.

The arrivals had occurred long before, then during, and long after the Homecoming with no commingling of essences beyond the hearth or up the flue. They were as composed and sedate as cats, great feline things in no need of company or sustenance, for they fed upon themselves and were well sated sure.

Catwise indeed were they, with starts from the outer Hebrides or arousals in the China Seas, or much-hurried hurricanes flung hopeless from the Cape, or flurried south with freezing breaths to meet the breaths of fire that moved intemperately across the Gulf.

And thus it was the chimney flues in all the House were full-inhabited, with winds of memory that knew the oldest storms and told their frights if you but lit the logs below.

Or if the voice of Timothy shot up this flue or that, the Mystic Seaport winter would weep a tale, or London's fog in transit on a westerly would whisper, murmur, hiss lipless its unlit days and sightless nights.

All told there were then some ninety-nine, perhaps one hundred kindred spells of weather on the move, a tribe of temperatures, the ancient airs, the recent blows of hot and cold that, seeking, found good lodging where thus hidden they waited for a rain-soaked wind to cork them out to join carousals of fresh storm. The House then was a great vintage bin of muttered yelling, heard but not seen, opinions of pure air.

Sometimes when Timothy could not sleep he lay down on this hearth or that and called on up the flue to summon midnight company and speak the traveling of winds across the world. Then he knew company as down the brick-walled flues the spirit tales would drift in lightless snow to touch his ears, excite Arach's hysterias, palpitate the Mouse, and cause Anuba to sit up in feline recognition of strange friends.

And so it was the House was home to seen or most unseen, the rooms of Family walled in by comforters of breeze and wind and climates from all time and every place.

Invisibles in flues.

Rememberers of noons.

Tellers of sunsets lost in air.

The ninety-nine or one hundred chimneys, nothing in each.

Except *them*.

CHAPTER 20

The Traveler

Father looked into Cecy's attic-space just before dawn. She lay upon the riverbed sands, quietly. He shook his head and waved at her.

"Now, if you can tell me what good she does, lying there," he said, "I'll devour the crepe on our porch windows. Sleeping all night, eating breakfast, and then sleeping again all day."

"Oh, but she's helpful!" explained Mother, leading him downstairs away from Cecy's slumbering pale figure. "Why, she's one of the busiest members of the Family. What good are your brothers who sleep all day and do nothing?"

They glided down through the scent of black candles, the black crepe on the banister whispering as they passed.

"Well, we work nights," Father said. "Can we help it if we're—as you put it—old-fashioned?"

"Of course not. Everyone in the Family can't be of the age." She opened the cellar door and they stepped down in darkness. "It's really very lucky I don't have to sleep *at all*. If you were married to a night-sleeper, what a marriage! Each of us to our own. All wild. That's how the Family goes. Sometimes like Cecy, all mind; and then there's Uncle Einar, all wing; and then again there's Timothy, all calm and worldly normal. You, sleeping days. And me, awake all and all of my life. So Cecy shouldn't be too much to understand. She helps in a million ways. She sails her mind to the greengrocer's for me! Or occupies the butcher's head to see if he's fresh out of good cuts. She warns me when gossips threaten to visit and spoil the afternoon. She's a travel pomegranate full of flights!"

They paused in the cellar near a large empty mahogany bin. He settled himself in. "But if she'd only contribute more," he said. "I must insist that she find real work."

"Sleep on it," she said. "You may change your mind by sunset."

She shut the bin on him.

"Well," he said.

"Good morning, dear," she said.

"Good morning," he said, muffled, enclosed.

The sun rose. She hurried upstairs.

Cecy awoke from a deep dream of sleep.

She looked upon reality and decided her wild and special world was the very world she preferred and needed. The dim outlines of the dry desert attic were familiar, as were the sounds below in a House that was all stir and bustle and wing-flurry at sunset, but now at noon was still with that dead stillness that the ordinary world assumes. The sun was fixed in the sky and the Egyptian sands that were her dreaming bed only waited for her mind with a mysterious hand to touch and inscribe there the charting of her travels.

All this she sensed and knew, and so with a dreamer's smile she settled back with her long and beautiful hair as cushion to sleep and dream and in her dreams . . .

She traveled.

Her mind slipped over the flowered yard, the fields, the green hills, over the ancient drowsy streets of town, into the wind and past the moist depression of the ravine. All day she would fly and meander. Her mind would pop into dogs to sit, all bristles, and taste ripe bones, sniff tangy-urined trees to hear as dogs hear,

run as dogs run, all smiles. It was more than telepathy, up one flue and down another. It was entry to lazing cats, old lemony maids, hopscotch girls, lovers on morning beds, then unborn babes' pink, dream-small brains.

Where would she go today?

She decided.

She went!

At this very instant there burst into the silent House below a fury of madness. A man, a crazed uncle of such reputation as would cause all in the Family to start and pull back in their own midnights. An uncle from the times of the Transylvanian wars and a crazed lord of a dreadful manor who impaled his enemies on spikes thrust into their bowels to leave them suspended, thrashing in horrible deaths. This uncle, John the Unjust, had arrived from dark lower Europe some months past only to discover there was no room for his decayed persona and his dreadful past. The Family was strange, perhaps outré, in some degree rococo, but not a scourge, a disease, an annihilation such as he represented with crimson eye, razored teeth, taloned claw, and the voice of a million impaled souls.

A moment after his mad burst into the noon-quiet House, empty save for Timothy and his mother who stood guard while the others slept under threat by the sun, John the Terrible elbowed them out of the way and ascended with ravening voice to rage the dreaming sands around Cecy, causing a Sahara storm about her peace.

"Damn!" he cried. "Is she here? Am I too late?"

"Get back," said the dark mother rising in the attic confines with Timothy near. "Are you blind? She's gone and might not be back for days!"

John the Terrible, the Unjust, kicked the sands at the sleeping maid. He seized her wrist to find a hidden pulse. "Damn!" he cried again. "Call her back. I *need* her!"

"You heard me!" Mother moved forward. "She's not to be touched. She's got to be left as she is."

Uncle John turned his head. His long hard red face was pocked and senseless.

"Where'd she go? I *must* find her!"

Mother spoke quietly. "You might find her in a child running in the ravine. You might find her in a crayfish under a rock in the creek. Or she might be playing chess behind an old man's face in the courthouse square." A wry look touched the mother's mouth. "She might be here now, looking out at you, laughing, not telling. This might be her talking with great fun."

"Why—" He swung heavily around. "If I *thought*—"

Mother continued, quietly. "Of course she's *not* here. And if she was, there'd be no way to tell." Her eyes gleamed with a delicate malice. "Why do you need her?"

He listened to a distant bell, tolling. He shook his head, angrily.

"Something . . . inside . . ." He broke off. He leaned over her warm, sleeping body. "Cecy! Come back! You can if you want!"

The wind blew softly outside the sun-feathered windows. The sand drifted under her quiet arms. The distant bell tolled again and he listened to the drowsy summer-day sound of it, far, far away.

"I've worked for her. The past month, awful thoughts. I was going to take the train to the city for help. But Cecy can catch these fears. She can clean the cobwebs, make me new. You see? She's *got* to help!"

"After all you've done to the Family?" said Mother.

"I did nothing!"

"When we had no room here, when we were full to the gables, you swore at us—"

"You have always hated me!"

"We feared you, perhaps. You have a history that is dreadful."

"No reason to turn me away!"

"Much reason. Nevertheless, if there had been room—"

"Lies. Lies!"

"Cecy wouldn't help you. The Family wouldn't approve."

"Damn the Family!"

"*You* have damned them. Some have disappeared in the past month since our refusal. You have been gossiping in town; it's only a matter of time before they might come after us."

"They might! I drink and talk. Unless you help, I might drink more. These damned bells! Cecy can stop them."

"These bells," said the lonely wraith of a woman. "When did they begin? How long have you heard them?"

"Long?" He paused and rolled his eyes back as if to see. "Since you locked me out. Since I went and—" He froze.

"Drank and talked too much and made the winds blow the wrong way around our roofs?"

"I did no such thing!"

"It's in your face. You speak one thing and threaten another."

"Hear this, then," John the Terrible said. "Listen, dreamer." He stared at Cecy. "If you don't return by sunset, to shake my mind, clear my head . . ."

"You have a list of all our dearest souls, which you will revise and publish with your drunken tongue?"

"*You* said it, *I* didn't."

He stopped, eyes shut. The distant bell, the holy, holy bell was tolling again. It tolled, it tolled, it tolled.

He shouted over its sound. "You heard me!"

He reared to plunge out of the attic.

His heavy shoes pounded away, down the stairs. When the noises were gone, the pale woman turned to look, quietly, at the sleeper.

"Cecy," she called softly. "Come home!"

There was only silence. Cecy lay, not moving, for as long as her mother waited.

John the Terrible, the Unjust, strode through the fresh open country and into the streets of town, searching for her in every child that licked an ice pop and in every small white dog that padded by on its way to some eagerly anticipated nowhere.

Uncle John stopped to wipe his face with his handkerchief. I'm afraid, he thought. Afraid.

He saw a code of birds strung dot-dash on the high telephone wires. Was she up there laughing at him with sharp bird eyes, shuffling feathers, singing?

Distantly, as on a sleepy Sunday morning, he heard the bells ringing in a valley in his head. He stood in blackness where pale faces drifted.

"Cecy!" he cried, to everything, everywhere. "I know you can help! Shake me! Shake me!"

Standing with the downtown cigar store Indian for conversation, John shook his head violently.

What if he never found her? What if the winds had borne her off to Elgin where she dearly loved to bide her time? The asylum for the insane, might she now be touching and turning their confetti thoughts?

Far-flung in the afternoon a great metal whistle sighed and echoed; steam shuffled as a train cut across valley trestles, over cool rivers through ripe cornfields, into tunnels, under arches of shimmering walnut trees. John stood, afraid. What if Cecy hid in the cabin of the engineer's head? She loved riding the monster engines. Yank the whistle rope to shriek across sleeping night land or drowsy day country.

He walked along a shady street. From the corners of his eyes he thought he saw an old woman, wrinkled as a fig, naked as a thistle-seed, among the branches of a hawthorn tree, a cedar stake driven in her chest.

Something screamed and thumped his head. A blackbird, soaring, snatched his hair.

"Damn!"

He saw the bird circle, awaiting another chance.

He heard a whirring sound.

He grabbed.

He had the bird! It squalled in his hands.

"Cecy!" he cried at his caged fingers and the wild black creature. "Cecy, I'll kill you if you don't help!"

The bird shrieked.

He closed his fingers tight, tight!

He walked away from where he dropped the dead thing and did not look back.

He walked down into the ravine and on the creek bank he laughed to think of the Family scurrying madly, trying to find some escape from him.

BB-shot eyes lay deep in the water, staring up.

On blazing hot summer noons, Cecy had often entered into the soft-shelled grayness of the mandibled heads of crayfish, peeking from the black egg eyes on their sensitive filamentary stalks to feel the creek sluice, steadily, in veils of coolness and captured light.

The realization that she might be near, in squirrels or chipmunks, or even . . . my god, think!

On sweltering summer noons, Cecy would thrive in amoebae, vacillating, deep in the philosophical dark waters of a kitchen well. On days when the world was a dreaming nightmare of heat printed on each object of the land, she'd lie, quivering, cool, and distant, in the well-throat.

John stumbled, fell flat into the creek water.

The bells rang louder. And now, one by one, a procession of bodies seemed to float by. Worm-white creatures drifting like marionettes. Passing, the tide bobbed their heads so their faces rolled, revealing the features of the Family.

He began to weep, sitting in the water. Then he stood up, shaking, and walked out of the creek and up the hill. There was only one thing to do.

John the Unjust, the Terrible, staggered into the police station in the late afternoon, barely able to stand, his voice a retching whisper.

The sheriff took his feet down off his desk and waited for the wild man to gain his breath and speak.

"I am here to report a family," he gasped. "A family of sin and wickedness who abide, who hide, seen but unseen, here, there, nearby."

The sheriff sat up. "A family? And wicked, you say?" He picked up a pencil. "Just where?"

"They live—" The wild man stopped. Something had struck him in the chest. Blinding lights burned his eyes. He swayed.

"Could you give me a name?" said the sheriff, mildly curious.

"Their name—" Again a terrific blow struck his midriff. The church bells *exploded*!

"Your voice, my god, your voice!" cried John.

"My voice?"

"It sounds like—" John pushed his hand out toward the sheriff's face. "Like—"

"Yes?"

"It's *her* voice. She's behind your eyes, back of your face, on your tongue!"

"Fascinating," said the sheriff, smiling, his voice terribly soft and sweet. "You were going to give me a name, a family, a place—"

"No use. If she's here. If your tongue is her tongue. Gods!"

"Try," said the fine and gentle voice inside the sheriff's face.

"The Family *is*!" cried the staggering, raving man. "The House *is*!" He fell back, struck again in his heart. The bells roared. The church bells wielded him as iron clapper.

He cried a name. He shouted a place.

Then, riven, he lunged out of the office.

After a long moment the sheriff's face relaxed. His voice changed. Low now and brusque, he seemed stunned in recall.

"What," he asked himself, "did someone say? Damn, damn. What was that name? Quick, write it down. And that house? *Where* did someone say?"

He looked at his pencil.

"Oh, yeah," he said at last. And again, "Yeah."

The pencil moved. He wrote.

The trapdoor to the attic burst upward and the terrible, the unjust man was there. He stood over Cecy's dreaming body.

"The bells," he said, his hands to his ears. "They're yours! I should've known. Hurting me, punishing me. Stop! We'll burn you! I'll bring the mob. Oh God, my head!"

With one last crushing gesture he crammed his fist to his ears and dropped dead.

The lonely woman of the House moved to look down at the body while Timothy, in the shadows, felt his companions panic and twitch and hide.

"Oh, Mother," said Cecy's quiet voice from her wakened lips. "I tried to stop him. Didn't. He named our name, he said our place. Will the sheriff remember?"

The lonely woman of midnights had no answer.

Timothy, in the shadows, listened.

From Cecy's lips far off and now near and clear came the soundings of the bells, the bells, the awful holy bells.

The sounding of the bells.

CHAPTER 21

Return to the Dust

Timothy stirred in his sleep.

The nightmare came and would not go away.

Within his head the roof caught fire. The windows trembled and broke. Throughout the great House wings shivered and flew, beating against the panes until they shattered.

Crying out, Timothy sat bolt upright. Almost immediately one word and then a tumble of words spilled from his lips:

"Nef. Dust witch. Great Times A Thousand Times Grandmère . . . Nef . . ."

She was calling him. There was silence, yet she called.

She knew the fire and the wild beating of wings and the broken panes.

He sat for a long while before he moved.

"Nef . . . dust . . . A Thousand Times Great Grand-mère . . ."

Born into death two thousand years before the crown of thorns, the Gethsemane garden, and the empty tomb. Nef, mother to Nefertiti, the royal mummy who drifted on a dark boat past the deserted Mount of the Sermon, scraped over the Rock at Plymouth and land-sailed to Little Fort in upper Illinois, surviving Grant's twilight assaults and Lee's pale dawn retreats. Seated for funeral celebrations by the Family Dark she was, over time, stashed from room to room, floor to floor, until this small hemp-rope, tobacco-leaf-brown, ancestral relic was lifted, light as balsa wood, to the upper attics where she was covered, smothered, then ignored by a Family eager for survival and forgetful of unremembered deaths' leftovers.

Abandoned to attic silence and the drift of golden pollens on the air, sucking in darkness as sustenance, breathing out only quiet and serenity, this ancient visitor waited for someone to pull aside the accumulated love letters, toys, melted candles and candelabras, tattered skirts, corsets, and headlined papers from wars won-then-lost in instantly neglectful Pasts.

Someone to dig, rifle, and find.

Timothy.

He had not visited her in months. Months. Oh Nef, he thought.

Nef from the mysterious isle arose because he came and leafed, dug, and tossed aside until just her face, her sewn-shut eyes were framed in autumn book leaves, legal tracts, and jackstraw mouse bones.

"Grandmère!" he cried. "Forgive me!"

"Not . . . so . . . loud . . ." whispered her voice, a ventriloquist's thrown syllables from four thousand years of quiet echoes. "You . . . will . . . shatter . . . me."

And indeed platelets of dry sand fell from her bandaged shoulders, hieroglyphs tattered on her breastplate.

"Look . . ."

A tiny spiral of dust brushed along her ciphered bosom where gods of life and death posed as stiffly as tall rows of ancient corn and wheat.

Timothy's eyes grew wide.

"That." He touched the face of a child sprung up in a field of holy beasts. "Me?"

"Indeed."

"Why did you call me?"

"Be . . . cause . . . it . . . is . . . the . . . end." The slow words fell like golden crumbs from her lips.

A rabbit thumped and ran in Timothy's chest.

"End of *what*!?"

One of the sewn eyelids of the ancient woman opened the merest crack to show a crystal gleam tucked within. Timothy glanced up at the attic beams where that gleam touched its light.

"This?" he said. "*Our* place?"

". . . Yesssss . . ." came the whisper. She sewed one eyelid back up, but opened the other with light.

Her fingers, trembling across her bosom pictographs, touched like a spider as she whispered:

"This . . ."

Timothy responded. "Uncle Einar!"

"He who has wings?"

"I've *flown* with him."

"Rare child. And *this*?"

"Cecy!"

"She also flies?"

"With no wings. She sends her mind—"

"Like ghosts?"

"Which use people's ears to look out their eyes!"

"And this?" The spider fingers trembled.

There was no symbol where she pointed.

"Ah," Timothy laughed. "My cousin, Ran. Invisible. Doesn't *need* to fly. Can go anywhere and no one knows."

"Fortunate man. And this and this and yet again *this*?"

Her dry finger moved and scratched.

And Timothy named all of the uncles and aunts and cousins and nieces and nephews who had lived in this House forever, or a hundred years, give or take bad weather, storms, or war. There were thirty rooms and each more filled with cobwebs and nightbloom and sneezes of ectoplasms that posed in mirrors to be blown away when death's-head moths or funeral dragonflies sewed the air and flung the shutters wide to let the dark spill in.

Timothy named each hieroglyphic face and the ancient woman gave the merest nod of her dusty head as her fingers lay on a final hieroglyph.

"Do I touch the maelstrom of darkness?"

"This House, yes."

And it was so. There lay this very House, embossed with lapis lazuli and trimmed with amber and gold, as it must have been when Lincoln went unheard at Gettysburg.

And as he gazed, the bright embossments began to shiver and flake. An earthquake shook the frames and blinded the golden windows.

"Tonight," mourned the dust, turned in on itself.

"But," cried Timothy, "after so long. Why *now*?"

"It is the age of discovery and revelations. The pictures that fly through the air. The sounds that blow in the winds. Things seen by many. Things heard by all. Travelers on the road by the tens of millions. No escape. We have been found by the words in the air and the pictures sent on light beams into rooms where children and children's parents sit while Medusa, with insect-antenna coif, tells all and seeks punishment."

"For what?"

"No reason is needed. It is just the revelation of the hour, the meaningless alarms and excursions of the week, the panic of the single night, no one asks, but death and destruction are delivered, as the children sit with their parents behind them, frozen in an arctic spell of unwanted gossip and unneeded slander. No matter. The dumb will speak, the stupid will assume, and we are destroyed.

"Destroyed . . ." she echoed.

And the House on her bosom and the House beams above the boy shook, waiting for more quakes.

"The floods will soon arrive . . . inundations. Tidal waters of men . . ."

"But what have we done?"

"Nothing. We have survived, is all. And those who come to drown us are envious of our lives lived for so many centuries. Because we are different, we must be washed away. Hist!"

And again her hieroglyphs shook and the attic sighed and creaked like a ship in a rising sea.

"What can we do?" Timothy asked.

"Escape to all directions. They cannot follow so many flights. The House must be vacant by midnight, when they will come with torches."

"Torches?"

"Isn't it always fire and torches, torches and fire?"

"Yes." Timothy felt his tongue move, stunned with remembrance. "I have seen films. Poor running people, people running after. And torches and fire."

"Well then. Call your sister. Cecy must warn all the rest."

"This I have done!" cried a voice from nowhere.

"Cecy!?"

"She is with us," husked the old woman.

"Yes! I've heard it all," said the voice from the beams, the window, the closets, the downward stairs. "I am in every room, in every thought, in every head. Already the bureaus are being ransacked, the luggage packed. Long before midnight, the House will be empty."

A bird unseen brushed Timothy's eyelids and ears and settled behind his gaze to blink out at Nef.

"Indeed, the Beautiful One is here," said Cecy in Timothy's throat and mouth.

"Nonsense! Would you hear another reason why the weather will change and the floods come?" said the ancient.

"Indeed." Timothy felt the soft presence of his sister press against his windowed eyes. "Tell us, Nef."

"They hate me because I am the accumulation of the knowledge of Death. That knowledge is a curse to them instead of a useful burden."

"Can," started Timothy, and Cecy finished, "can death be remembered?"

"Oh, yes. But only by the dead. You the living are blind. But we who have bathed in Time, and been reborn as children of the earth and inheritors of Eternity, drift gently in rivers of sand and streams of darkness, knowing the bombardment from the stars whose emanations have taken millions of years to rain upon the land and seek us out in our plantations of eternally wrapped souls like great seeds beneath the marbled layers and the bas-relief skeletons of reptile birds that fly on sandstone, with wingspreads a million years wide and as deep as a single breath. We are the keepers of Time. You who walk the earth know only the moment, which is whisked away with your next exhalation. Because you move and live, you cannot keep. We are the granaries of dark remembrance. Our funerary jars keep not only our lights and silent hearts, but our wells, deeper than you can imagine, where in the subterranean lost hours, all the deaths that ever were, the deaths on which mankind has built new tenements of flesh and ramparts of stone moving ever upward even as we sink down and down, doused in twilights, bandaged by midnights. We accumulate. We are wise with farewells. Would you not admit, child, that forty billion deaths are a great wisdom, and those forty billion who shelve under the earth are a great gift to the living so that they might live?"

"I guess."

"Do not guess, child. *Know*. I will teach, and that knowledge, important to living because only death can set the world free to be born again—that is your sweet burden. And tonight is the night when your task begins. *Now!*"

At which moment, the bright medal in the center of her golden breast flared. The light blazed up to swarm the ceiling like a thousand summer bees threatening, by their very flash and friction, to fire the dry beams. The attic seemed to spin with the rush-around light and heat. Every slat, shingle, crossbeam groaned and expanded, while Timothy raised his arms and hands to ward off the swarms, staring at the kindled bosom of Nef.

"Fire!" he cried. "Torches!"

"Yes," hissed the old, old woman. "Torches and fire. Nothing stays. All burns."

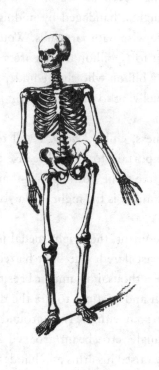

And with this, the architecture of the long-before-Gettysburg-and-Appomattox House smoked on her breastplate.

"Nothing stays!" cried Cecy, everywhere at once, like the fireflies and summer bees bumping to char the beams. "All goes!"

And Timothy blinked and bent to watch the winged man, and the sleeping Cecy, and the Unseen Uncle (invisible save for his passing like the wind through clouds or snowstorms, or wolves running in fields of black wheat, or bats in wounded zigzag flights devouring the moon), and a double dozen of other aunts and uncles and cousins striding the road away from town. Or soaring, to lodge in trees a mile off and safe, as the mob, the torchlit madness, flowed up old Nef-Mum's chest. Off out the window Timothy could see the real mob coming with torches, heading toward the House like a backward flow of lava, on foot, bike, and car, a storm of cries choking their throats.

Even as Timothy felt the floorboards shift, like a scale from which weights are dropped, with seventy times a hundred pounds in flight they jumped overboard from porches. The House skeleton, shaken free, grew tall as winds vacuumed the now-empty rooms and flapped the ghost curtains and sucked the front door wide to welcome the torches and fire and the crazed mob.

"All goes," cried Cecy, a final time.

And she abandoned their eyes and ears and bodies and minds and, restored to her body below, ran so lightly, quickly, her feet left no tread in the grass.

There was a storm of activity. All around the House things were happening. Air was rushing up the flue of the chimneys. Ninety-nine or one hundred chimneys were all sighing or moaning and mourning at the same time. Shingles seemed to be flying off the roof. There was a great fluttering of wings. There was a sound of much weeping. All the rooms were being emptied. In the middle of all this excitement, all this activity, all this flurry, Timothy heard Great Grandmère say:

"What now, Timothy?"

"What?"

She said, "In another hour the House will be empty. You will be here alone and getting ready to make a long journey. I want to go with you on your travels. Maybe we won't be able to speak much along the way, but before we go, in the midst of all this, I want to ask you, do you still want to be like us?"

Timothy thought for a long moment and then said, "Well—"

"Speak up. I know your thoughts, but you must speak them."

"No, I don't want to be like you," said Timothy.

"Is this the beginning of wisdom?" Grandmère said.

"I don't know. I've been thinking. I've been watching all of you and I decided that maybe I want to have a life just like people have always had. I want to know that I was born and I guess that I have to accept the fact that I must die. But watching you, seeing all of you, I see that all these long years haven't made any difference."

"What do you mean?" said Great Grandmère.

A great wind rushed by, sparks flew, singeing her dried wrappings.

"Well, are you all happy? I wonder about that. I feel very sad. Some nights I wake up and cry because I realize that you have all this time, all these years, but there doesn't seem to be much that's very happy that came of it all."

"Ah, yes, Time is a burden. We know too much, we remember too much. We have indeed lived too long. The best thing to do, Timothy, in your new wisdom is to live your life to the fullest, enjoy every moment, and lay yourself down, many years from now, happily realizing that you've filled every moment, every hour, every year of your life and that you are much loved by the Family. Now, let us get ready to leave.

"And now," wheezed old Nef, "you be my savior, child. Lift and carry."

"Can't!" cried Timothy.

"I am dandelion seed and thistledown. Your breath will drift, your heartbeat, sustain me. Now!"

And it was so. With one exhalation, a touch of his hands, the wrapped gift from long before Saviors and the parted Red Sea arose on the air. And seeing he could carry this parcel of dream and bones, Timothy wept and ran.

In the upheaval of wings and scarves of spirit illumination the swift passage of lightless clouds over the valleys in tumult caused such an upthrust suction that all of the chimneys, ninety-nine or one hundred, exhaled, shrieked, and let gasp a great outburst of soot and wind from the Hebrides, and air from the far Tortugas, and cyclone layabouts from nowhere Kansas. This erupted volcano of tropic and then arctic air struck and cracked the clouds to pummel them into a shower and then a downpour and then a Johnstown flood of drenching rain that quenched the fire and blackened the House in half ruin.

And while the House was being battered and drowned the downpour so smothered the rage in the mob that it pulled back in sudden clots, slogged about, trailing water, and dispersed on home, leaving the storm to rinse the facade of the empty shell, while there remained one great hearth and chimney which sounded its throat up to where a miraculous residue hung almost upon looms of nothing, sustained by no more than a few timbers and a sleeping breath.

There lay Cecy, quietly smiling at tumults, signaling the thousand Family members to fly here, amble there, let wind lift you, let earth gravitate you down, be leaf, be web, be hoofless print, be lipless smile, be mouthless fang, be boneless pelt, be shroud of mist at dawn, be souls invisible from chimney throats, all list and listen, go, you east, you west, nest trees, bed meadow grass, hitch ride of larks, dog-track with dogs, make cats to care, find bucket wells to lurk, dent farmland beds and pillows with no shape of heads, wake dawns with hummingbirds, hive snug with sunset bees, list, list, all!

And the last of the rain gave the charred shell of House a final rinse and ceased and there were only dying smokes and half a House with half a heart and half a lung and Cecy there, a compass to their dreams, forever signaling their rampant destinations.

There went all and everyone in a flow of dreams to faraway hamlets and forests and farms, and Mother and Father with them in a blizzard of whispers and prayers, calling farewell, promising returns in some future year, so to seek and hold once again their abandoned son. Goodbye, goodbye, oh yea, goodbye, their fading voices cried. Then all was silence save for Cecy beckoning more melancholy farewells.

And all this, Timothy perceived and tearfully knew.

From a mile beyond the House, which now glowed

with sparks and plumes to darken the sky, to storm-cloud the moon, Timothy stopped under a tree where many of his cousins and perhaps Cecy caught their breath, even as a rickety jalopy braked and a farmer peered out at the distant blaze and the nearby child.

"What's that?" He pointed his nose at the burning House.

"Wish I knew," said Timothy.

"What you *carrying,* boy?"

The man scowled at the long bundle under Timothy's arm.

"Collect 'em," said Timothy. "Old newspapers. Comic strips. Old magazines. Headlines, heck, some before the Rough Riders. Some before Bull Run. Trash and junk." The bundle under his arm rustled in the night wind. "Great junk, swell trash."

"Just like me, once." The farmer laughed quietly. "No more. Need a ride?"

Timothy nodded. He looked back at the House, saw sparks like fireflies shooting into the night sky.

"Get in."

And they drove away.

CHAPTER 22

The One Who Remembers

For a long while, many days and then weeks, the place was empty above the town. On occasion when the rains came and the lightning struck, the merest plume of smoke would arise from the charred timbers sunk inward on the cellar and its broken vintages and from the attic beams fallen in black skeletons on themselves to cover the buried wines. When there was no longer smoke there was dust which lifted in veils and clouds, in which visions, remembrances of the House, flickered and faded like sudden starts of dream, and then these, too, ceased.

And with the passage of time a young man came

along the road like one emerging from a dream or stepping forth from the quiet tides along a silent sea to find himself in a strange landscape staring at the abandoned House as if he knew but did not know what it had once contained.

The wind shifted in the empty trees, questioning.

He listened carefully and replied:

"Tom," he said. "It's Tom. Do you know me? Do you remember?"

The branches of the tree trembled with remembrance.

"Are you here now?" he said.

Almost, came the whisper of a reply. *Yes. No.*

The shadows stirred.

The front door of the House squealed and slowly blew open. He moved to the bottom of the steps leading up.

The chimney flue at the center of the House hollowed a breath of temperate weather.

"If I go in and wait, then what?" he said, watching the vast front of the silent House for response.

The front door drifted on its hinges. The few remaining windows shook softly in their frames, reflecting the first twilight stars.

He heard but did not hear the sussurance about his ears.

Go in. Wait.

He put his foot on the bottom step and hesitated.

The timbers of the House leaned away from him as if to draw him near.

He took another step.

"I don't know. What? Who am I looking for?"

Silence. The House waited. The wind waited in the trees.

"Ann? Is *that* who? But no. She's long gone away. But there was another. I *almost* know her name. What . . . ?"

The House timbers groaned with impatience. He moved up to the third step and then all the way to the top where he stood, imbalanced by the wide open door where the weather drew its breath, as if to waft him in. But he stood very still, eyes shut, trying to see a shadow face behind his eyelids.

I almost know the name, he thought.

In. In.

He stepped in through the door.

Almost instantly the House sank the merest quarter of an inch as if the night had come upon it or a cloud drifted to weight the high attic roof.

In the attic heights there was a dream inside of a slumber inside of a flesh.

"Who's there?" he called quietly. "Where are you?"

The attic dust rose and sank in a stir of shadow.

"Oh, yes, yes," he said at last. "I know it now. Your blessed name."

He moved to the bottom of the stairs leading up through the moonlight to the waiting attic of the House.

He took a breath.

"Cecy," he said, at last.

The House trembled.

Moonlight shone on the stairs.

He went up.

"Cecy," he said a final time.

The front door slowly, slowly drifted and then slid and then very quietly shut.

CHAPTER 23

The Gift

There was a tap at the door and Dwight William Alcott looked up from a display of photographs just sent on from some digs outside Karnak. He was feeling especially well fed, visually, or he would not have answered the tap. He nodded, which seemed signal enough, for the door opened immediately and a bald head moved in.

"I know this is curious," said his assistant, "but there is a child here . . ."

"That *is* curious," said D. W. Alcott. "Children do not usually come here. He has no appointment?"

"No, but he insists that after you see the gift he has for you, you'll make an appointment, *then*."

"An unusual way to make appointments," mused Alcott. "Should I see this child? A boy, is it?"

"A brilliant boy, so he tells me, bearing an ancient treasure."

"That's too much for me!" The curator laughed. "Let him in."

"I already am." Timothy, half inside the door, scuttled forward with a great rattling of stuffs under his arm.

"Sit down," said D. W. Alcott.

"If you don't mind, I'll stand. She might want two chairs, sir, however."

"*Two* chairs?"

"If you don't mind, sir."

"Bring an extra chair, Smith."

"Yes, sir."

And two chairs were brought and Timothy lifted the long balsa-light gift and placed it on both chairs where the bundled stuffs shown in a good light.

"Now, young man—"

"Timothy," supplied the boy.

"Timothy, I'm busy. State your business, please."

"Yes, sir."

"Well?"

"Four thousand four hundred years and nine hundred million deaths, sir . . ."

"My God, that's quite a mouthful." D. W. Alcott

waved at Smith. "Another chair." The chair was brought. "Now you really must sit down, son." Timothy sat. "Say that again."

"I'd rather not, sir. It sounds like a lie."

"And yet," said D. W. Alcott, slowly, "why do I believe you?"

"I have that kind of face, sir."

The curator of the museum leaned forward to study the pale and intense face of the boy.

"By God," he murmured, "you *do*."

"And what have we here?" he went on, nodding to what appeared to be a catafalque. "You know the *name* papyrus?"

"Everyone knows *that*."

"Boys, I suppose. Having to do with robbed tombs and Tut. Boys know papyrus."

"Yes, sir. Come look, if you want."

The curator *wanted*, for he was already on his feet.

He arrived to look down and probe as through a filing cabinet, leaf by leaf of cured tobacco, it almost seemed, with here and there the head of a lion or the body of a hawk. Then his fingers riffled faster and faster and he gasped as if struck in the chest.

"Child," he said and let out another breath. "Where did you find these?"

"*This*, not these, sir. And I didn't find it, it found *me*.

Hide and seek in a way, it said. I heard. Then it wasn't hidden anymore."

"My God," gasped D.W. Alcott, using both hands now to open "wounds" of brittle stuff. "Does this belong to you?"

"It works both ways, sir. It owns me, I own it. We're family."

The curator glanced over at the boy's eyes. "Again," he said, "I *do* believe."

"Thank God."

"Why do you thank God?"

"Because if you didn't believe me, I'd have to leave." The boy edged away.

"No, no," cried the curator. "No need. But why do you speak as if this, *it*, owned you, as if you are related?"

"Because," said Timothy. "It's Nef, sir."

"Nef?"

Timothy reached over and folded back a tissue of bandage.

From deep under the openings of papyrus, the sewn-shut eyes of the old, old woman could be seen, with a hidden creek of vision between the lids. Dust filtered from her lips.

"Nef, sir," said the boy. "Mother of Nefertiti."

The curator wandered back to his chair and reached for a crystal decanter.

"Do you drink wine, boy?"

"Not until today, sir."

Timothy sat for a long moment, waiting, until Mr. D. W. Alcott handed him a small glass of wine. They drank together and at last Mr. D. W. Alcott said:

"Why have you brought this—it—her here?"

"It's the only safe place in the world."

The curator nodded. "True. Are you offering," he paused. "Nef? For sale?"

"No, sir."

"What do you want, then?"

"Just that if she stays here, sir, that once a day, you talk to her." Embarrassed, Timothy looked at his shoes.

"Would you trust me to do that, Timothy?"

Timothy looked up. "Oh, yes, sir. If you *promised*."

Then he went on, raising his gaze to fix on the curator.

"More than that, *listen* to her."

"She talks, does she?"

"A lot, sir."

"Is she talking, now?"

"Yes, but you have to bend close. I'm used to it, now. After a while, you will be, too."

The curator shut his eyes and listened. There was a rustle of ancient paper, somewhere, which wrinkled his face, listening. "What?" he asked. "What is it she, mainly, says?"

"Everything there is to say about death, sir."

"Everything?"

"Four thousand four hundred years, like I said, sir. And nine hundred million people who had to die so we can live."

"That's a lot of dying."

"Yes, sir. But I'm glad."

"What a terrible thing to say!"

"No, sir. Because if *they* were alive, we wouldn't be able to move. Or breathe."

"I see what you mean. She knows all *that*, does she?"

"Yes, sir. Her daughter was the Beautiful One Who Was There. So *she* is the One Who Remembers."

"The ghost that tells a flesh and soul complete history of the Book of the Dead?"

"I think so, sir. And one other thing," added Timothy.

"And?"

"If you don't mind, anytime I want, a visitor's card."

"So you can come visit anytime?"

"After hours, even."

"I think that can be arranged, son. There will be papers to be signed, of course, and authentication carried out."

The boy nodded.

The man rose.

"Silly of me to ask. Is she still talking?"

"Yes, sir. Come close. No, *closer*."

The boy nudged the man's elbow, gently.

Far off, near the temple of Karnak, the desert winds sighed. Far off, between the paws of a great lion, the dust settled.

"Listen," said Timothy.

How the Family Gathered

Where do I get my ideas and how long does it take to write an idea once I get it? Fifty-five years or nine days.

In the case of *From the Dust Returned*, the material started in 1945 and was only finished after a period stretching until 2000.

With *Fahrenheit 451*, I got the idea on a Monday and finished writing the first short version nine days later.

So you see, it all depends on the immediate passion. *Fahrenheit 451* was unusual and written during unusual times: that period of witch-hunting that ended with Joseph McCarthy in the fifties.

The Elliott family in *From the Dust Returned* began

living in my childhood when I was seven years old. When Halloween came each year my Aunt Neva piled me and my brother into her old tin lizzie to motor out into October Country to gather cornstalks and field pumpkins. We brought them to my grandparents' home and stocked pumpkins in every corner, put cornstalks on the porch, and placed the leaves from the dining room table on the staircases so that you had to slide instead of stepping down.

She stashed me in the attic clad as a witch with a wax nose, hid my brother at the bottom of a ladder leading up to the attic, and invited her Halloween celebrants to climb up through the night to enter our house. The atmosphere was rampant and hilarious. Some of my finest memories are of this magical aunt, only ten years older than myself.

Out of this background of uncles and aunts and my grandmother, I began to see that some of it should be caught on paper to be kept forever. So in my early twenties I began to jigger the idea of this Family who were most strange, outré, rococo—who could be, but maybe were not, vampires.

At the time I finished the first story about this remarkable household, in my early twenties, I was writing for *Weird Tales* magazine for the magnificent sum of a half-cent a word. I published many of my early stories there, not realizing that I was turning out tales that would out-last the magazine, far into today.

When I got a raise to a penny a word I thought I was rich. So my stories appeared, one by one, and I sold them for fifteen dollars, twenty dollars, sometimes twenty-five dollars apiece.

When I finished "Homecoming," the first story about my Family, *Weird Tales* promptly rejected it. I had been having trouble with them all along because they com-plained that my stories were not about traditional ghosts. They wanted graveyards, late nights, strange walkers, and amazing murders.

I could not raise Marley's ghost again and again, as much as I loved him and all the ghosts that haunted Scrooge. *Weird Tales* desired first cousins to Edgar Allan Poe's Amontillado or Washington Irving's thrown pumpkin head.

I simply couldn't do that; I tried again and again but along the way my stories turned into tales of men who discovered the skeleton inside themselves and were terri-fied of that skeleton. Or stories about jars full of strange unguessed creatures. *Weird Tales* accepted some of these stories, reluctantly, with complaints. So when "Home-coming" arrived at their offices they cried "Enough!" and the story came back. I didn't know what to do with it at that time because there were very few markets in the

United States for such tale telling. On a hunch I sent it to *Mademoiselle* magazine, where I'd had luck the year before selling a short story that I had submitted on impulse. Many months passed. I thought, well, perhaps the story had got lost. Finally I received a telegram from the editors, who said they had debated changing the story to fit the magazine, but instead they were going to change the magazine to fit the story!

They put together an entire October issue built around my "Homecoming" and got Kay Boyle and others to write October essays to round out the magazine. They hired the talents of Charles Addams, who was then an offbeat cartoonist for *The New Yorker,* and beginning to draw his own strange and wonderful "Addams Family." He created a remarkable two-page spread of my October House and my Family streaming through the autumn air and loping along the ground.

When the story finally appeared, I had grand meetings with Charles Addams in New York. We planned a collaboration: Over a period of years I would write more stories and Addams would illustrate them. Ultimately, we would gather them all, stories and drawings, into a book. The years passed, some stories were written, we stayed in touch but went our separate ways. My plans for a possible book were delayed by my good fortune in landing the job of writing the screenplay for John Huston's *Moby Dick*. But over the years, I kept revisiting my beloved Elliotts. That once-discrete tale, "Homecoming," became the cornerstone, a building block for the Life Story of the Elliott Family: their genesis and demise, their adventures and mishaps, their loves and their sorrows. By the time the last of these stories was written, dear Charles Addams had passed into that Eternity inhabited by the creatures of his and my world.

That, briefly, is the history of *From the Dust Returned*. Beyond this I might add that all my characters are based on the relatives who wandered through my grandmother's house on those October evenings when I was a child. My Uncle Einar was real, and the names of all the others in the book were once similarly attached to cousins or uncles or aunts. Though long dead, they live again and waft in the chimney flues, stairwells, and attics of my imagination, kept there with great love by this chap who was once fantastically young and incredibly impressed with the wonder of Halloween.

Recently, the nice folks at the Tee and Charles Addams Foundation sent me a copy of a letter I wrote to Charlie Addams in 1948—all about his wonderful painting of the "Homecoming" house, and the nascent plans we had to collaborate on an illustrated book. Dated February 11, 1948, the letter (written on my long-gone manual typewriter) reads, in part: ". . . let me say that I can't imagine putting out the book without you. . . . It will become a sort of Christmas Carol idea, Halloween after Halloween people will buy the book, just as they buy the Carol, to read at the fireplace, with lights low. Halloween is the time of year for story-telling. . . . I believe in this more than I have believed in anything in my writing career. I want you to be in it with me." Interestingly, my agent had been talking to William Morrow about the possibility of doing such a book, and so it is rather poetic, I think, that Morrow is publishing this book today, with Charlie's superb illustration on the cover. How I wish he were here to see this project come to fruition!

RAY BRADBURY
Summer 2000

The World of Ray Bradbury . . .

. . . is a marvelous, magical place, full of awesome wonders, delicious terrors, and the simplest of pleasures. We invite you to experience the storytelling genius of Ray Bradbury in the following selection of excerpts from some of his best known works. All you have to do is turn the page . . .

Dandelion Wine

Twelve-year-old Douglas Spaulding knows Green Town, Illinois, is as vast and deep as the whole wide world that lies beyond the city limits. It is a pair of brand-new tennis shoes, the first harvest of dandelions for Grandfather's renowned intoxicant, the distant clang of the trolley's bell on a hazy afternoon. It is yesteryear and tomorrow blended into an unforgettable always. But as young Douglas is about to discover, summer can be more than the repetition of established rituals whose mystical power holds time at bay. It can be a best friend moving away, a human time machine who can transport you back to the Civil War, or a sideshow automaton able to glimpse the bittersweet future.

It was a quiet morning, the town covered over with darkness and at ease in bed. Summer gathered in the weather, the wind had the proper touch, the breathing of the world was long and warm and slow. You had only to rise, lean from your window, and know that this indeed was the first real time of freedom and living, this was the first morning of summer.

Douglas Spaulding, twelve, freshly wakened, let summer idle him on its early-morning stream. Lying in his third-story cupola bedroom, he felt the tall power it gave him, riding high in the June wind, the grandest tower in town. At night, when the trees washed together, he flashed his gaze like a beacon from this lighthouse in all directions over swarming seas of elm and oak and maple. Now . . .

"Boy," whispered Douglas.

A whole summer ahead to cross off the calendar, day by day. Like the goddess Siva in the travel books, he saw his hands jump everywhere, pluck sour apples, peaches, and midnight plums. He would be clothed in trees and bushes and rivers. He would freeze, gladly, in the hoar-frosted ice-house door. He would bake, happily, with ten thousand chickens, in Grandma's kitchen.

But now—a familiar task awaited him.

One night each week he was allowed to leave his father, his mother, and his younger brother Tom asleep in their small house next door and run here, up the dark spiral stairs to his grandparents' cupola, and in this sorcerer's tower sleep with thunders and visions, to wake before the crystal jingle of milk bottles and perform his ritual magic.

He stood at the open window in the dark, took a deep breath and exhaled.

The street lights, like candles on a black cake, went out. He exhaled again and again and the stars began to vanish.

Douglas smiled. He pointed a finger.

There, and there. Now over here, and here . . .

Yellow squares were cut in the dim morning earth as house lights winked slowly on. A sprinkle of windows came suddenly alight miles off in dawn country.

"Everyone yawn. Everyone up."

The great house stirred below.

"Grandpa, get your teeth from the water glass!" He waited a decent interval. "Grandma and Great-grandma, fry hot cakes!"

The warm scent of fried batter rose in the drafty halls to stir the boarders, the aunts, the uncles, the visiting cousins, in their rooms.

"Street where all the Old People live, wake up! Miss Helen Loomis, Colonel Freeleigh, Miss Bentley! Cough, get up, take pills, move around! Mr. Jonas, hitch up your horse, get your junk wagon out and around!"

The bleak mansions across the town ravine opened baleful dragon eyes. Soon, in the morning avenues below, two old women would glide their electric Green Machine, waving at all the dogs. "Mr. Tridden, run to the carbarn!" Soon, scattering hot blue sparks above it, the town trolley would sail the rivering brick streets.

"Ready John Huff, Charlie Woodman?" whispered Douglas to the Street of Children. "Ready!" to baseballs sponged deep in wet lawns, to rope swings hung empty in trees.

"Mom, Dad, Tom, wake up."

Clock alarms tinkled faintly. The courthouse clock boomed. Birds leaped from trees like a net thrown by his hand, singing. Douglas, conducting an orchestra, pointed to the eastern sky.

The sun began to rise.

He folded his arms and smiled a magician's smile. Yes, sir, he thought, everyone jumps, everyone runs when I yell. It'll be a fine season.

He gave the town a last snap of his fingers.

Doors slammed open; people stepped out.

Summer 1928 began.

The Illustrated Man

Here are eighteen startling visions of humankind's destiny, unfolding across a canvas of decorated skin—visions as keen as the tattooist's needle and as colorful as the inks that indelibly stain the body. Ray Bradbury's The Illustrated Man is a kaleidoscopic blending of magic, imagination, and truth, widely believed to be one of the Grandmaster's premier accomplishments: as exhilarating as interplanetary travel, as maddening as a walk in a million-year rain, and as comforting as simple, familiar rituals on the last night of the world.

"Hey, the Illustrated Man!"

A calliope screamed, and Mr. William Philippus Phelps stood, arms folded, high on the summer-night platform, a crowd unto himself.

He was an entire civilization. In the Main Country, his chest, the Vasties lived—nipple-eyed dragons swirling over his fleshpot, his almost feminine breasts. His navel was the mouth of a slit-eyed monster—an obscene, in-sucked mouth, toothless as a witch. And there were secret caves where Darklings lurked, his armpits, adrip with slow subterranean liquors, where the Darklings, eyes jealously ablaze, peered out through rank creeper and hanging vine.

Mr. William Philippus Phelps leered down from his freak platform with a thousand peacock eyes. Across the sawdust meadow he saw his wife, Lisabeth, far away, ripping tickets in half, staring at the silver belt buckles of passing men.

Mr. William Philippus Phelps' hands were tattooed roses. At the sight of his wife's interest, the roses shriveled, as with the passing of sunlight.

A year before, when he had led Lisabeth to the marriage bureau to watch her work her name in ink, slowly, on the form, his skin had been pure and white and clean. He glanced down at himself in sudden horror. Now he was like a great painted canvas, shaken in the night wind! How had it happened? Where had it all begun?

It had started with the arguments, and then the flesh, and then the pictures. They had fought deep into the summer nights, she like a brass trumpet forever blaring at him. And he had gone out to eat five thousand steaming hot dogs, ten million hamburgers, and a forest of green onions, and to drink vast red seas of orange juice. Peppermint candy formed his brontosaur bones, the hamburgers shaped his balloon flesh, and strawberry pop pumped in and out of his heart valves sickeningly, until he weighed three hundred pounds.

"William Philippus Phelps," Lisabeth said to him in the eleventh month of their marriage, "you're dumb and fat."

That was the day the carnival boss handed him the blue envelope. "Sorry, Phelps. You're no good to me with all that gut on you."

"Wasn't I always your best tent man, boss?"

"Once. Not anymore. Now you sit, you don't get the work out."

"Let me be your Fat Man."

"I got a Fat Man. Dime a dozen." The boss eyed him up and down. "Tell you what, though. We ain't had a Tattooed Man since Gallery Smith died last year. . . ."

That had been a month ago. Four short weeks. From someone, he had learned of a tattoo artist far out in the rolling Wisconsin country, an old woman, they said, who knew her trade. If he took the dirt road and turned right at the river and then left . . .

He had walked out across a yellow meadow, which was crisp from the sun. Red flowers blew and bent in the wind as he walked, and he came to the old shack, which looked as if it had stood in a million rains.

Inside the door was a silent, bare room, and in the

center of the bare room sat an ancient woman.

Her eyes were stitched with red resin-thread. Her nose was sealed with black wax-twine. Her ears were sewn, too, as if a darning-needle dragonfly had stitched all her senses shut. She sat, not moving, in the vacant room. Dust lay in a yellow flour all about, unfootprinted in many weeks; if she had moved it would have shown, but she had not moved. Her hands touched each other like thin, rusted instruments. Her feet were naked and obscene as rain rubbers, and near them sat vials of tattoo milk—red, lightning-blue, brown, cat-yellow. She was a thing sewn tight into whispers and silence.

Only her mouth moved, unsewn: "Come in. Sit down. I'm lonely here."

The Martian Chronicles

Bradbury's Mars is a place of hope, dreams and metaphor—of crystal pillars and fossil seas—where a fine dust settles on the great, empty cities of a silently destroyed civilization. It is here the invaders have come to despoil and commercialize, to grow and to learn—first a trickle, then a torrent, rushing from a world with no future toward a promise of tomorrow. The Earthman conquers Mars . . . and then is conquered by it, lulled by dangerous lies of comfort and familiarity, and enchanted by the lingering glamour of an ancient, mysterious native race.

February 2030

Ylla

They had a house of crystal pillars on the planet Mars by the edge of an empty sea, and every morning you could see Mrs. K eating the golden fruits that grew from the crystal walls, or cleaning the house with handfuls of magnetic dust which, taking all dirt with it, blew away on the hot wind. Afternoons, when the fossil sea was warm and motionless, and the wine trees stood stiff in the yard, and the little distant Martian bone town was all enclosed, and no one drifted out their doors, you could see Mr. K himself in his room, reading from a metal book with raised hieroglyphs over which he brushed his hand, as one might play a harp. And from the book, as his fingers stroked, a voice sang, a soft ancient voice, which told tales of when the sea was red steam on the shore and ancient men had carried clouds of metal insects and electric spiders into battle.

Mr. and Mrs. K had lived by the dead sea for twenty years, and their ancestors had lived in the same house, which turned and followed the sun, flower-like, for ten centuries.

Mr. and Mrs. K were not old. They had the fair, brownish skin of the true Martian, the yellow coin eyes, the soft musical voices. Once they had liked painting pictures with chemical fire, swimming in the canals in the seasons when the wine trees filled them with green liquors, and talking into the dawn together by the blue phosphorous portraits in the speaking room.

They were not happy now.

This morning Mrs. K stood between the pillars, listening to the desert sands heat, melt into yellow wax, and seemingly run on the horizon.

Something was going to happen.

She waited.

She watched the blue sky of Mars as if it might at any moment grip in on itself, contract, and expel a shining miracle down upon the sand.

Nothing happened.

Tired of waiting, she walked through the misting pillars. A gentle rain sprang from the fluted pillar tops, cooling the scorched air, falling gently on her. On hot days it was like walking in a creek. The floors of the house glittered with cool streams. In the distance she heard her husband playing his book steadily, his fingers never tired of the old songs. Quietly she wished he might one day again spend as much time holding and touching her like a little harp as he did his incredible books.

But no. She shook her head, an imperceptible, forgiving shrug. Her eyelids closed softly down upon her golden eyes. Marriage made people old and familiar, while still young.

She lay back in a chair that moved to take her shape even as she moved. She closed her eyes tightly and nervously.

The dream occurred.

Her brown fingers trembled, came up, grasped at the air. A moment later she sat up, startled, gasping.

She glanced about swiftly, as if expecting someone there before her. She seemed disappointed; the space between the pillars was empty.

Her husband appeared in a triangular door. "Did you call?" he asked irritably.

"No!" she cried.

"I thought I heard you cry out."

"Did I? I was almost asleep and had a dream!"

"In the daytime? You don't often do that."

She sat as if struck in the face by the dream. "How strange, how very strange," she murmured. "The dream."

"Oh?" He evidently wished to return to his book.

"I dreamed about a man."

"A man?"

"A tall man, six feet one inch tall."

"How absurd; a giant, a misshapen giant."

"Somehow"—she tried the words—"he looked all right. In spite of being tall. And he had—oh, I know you'll think it silly—he had *blue* eyes!"

"Blue eyes! Gods!" cried Mr. K. "What'll you dream next? I suppose he had *black* hair?"

"How did you *guess*?" She was excited.

"I picked the most unlikely color," he replied coldly.

"Well, black it was!" she cried. "And he had a very white skin; oh, he was *most* unusual! He was dressed in a strange uniform and he came down out of the sky and spoke pleasantly to me." She smiled.

"Out of the sky; what nonsense!"

"He came in a metal thing that glittered in the sun," she remembered. She closed her eyes to shape it again. "I dreamed there was the sky and something sparkled like a coin thrown into the air, and suddenly it grew large and fell down softly to land, a long silver craft, round and alien. And a door opened in the side of the silver object and this tall man stepped out."

"If you worked harder you wouldn't have these silly dreams."

"I rather enjoyed it," she replied, lying back. "I never suspected myself of such an imagination. Black hair, blue eyes, and white skin! What a strange man, and yet—quite handsome."

"Wishful thinking."

"You're unkind. I didn't think him up on purpose; he just came in my mind while I drowsed. It wasn't like a dream. It was so unexpected and different. He looked at me and he said, 'I've come from the third planet in my ship. My name is Nathaniel York—'"

"A stupid name; it's no name at all," objected the husband.

"Of course it's stupid, because it's a dream," she explained softly. "And he said, 'This is the first trip across space. There are only two of us in our ship, myself and my friend Bert.'"

"*Another* stupid name."

"And he said, 'We're from a city on *Earth*; that's the name of our planet,'" continued Mrs. K. "That's what he said. 'Earth' was the name he spoke. And he used another language. Somehow I understood him. With my mind. Telepathy, I suppose."

The October Country

The October Country's *inhabitants live, dream, work, die—and sometimes live again—discovering, often too late, the high price of citizenship. Here a glass jar can hold memories and nightmares; a woman's newborn child can plot murder; and a man's skeleton can war against him. Here there is no escaping the dark stranger who lives upstairs . . . or the reaper who wields the world. Each of these stories is a wonder, imagined by an acclaimed tale-teller writing from a place of shadows.*

The Small Assassin

Just when the idea occurred to her that she was being murdered she could not tell. There had been little subtle signs, little suspicions for the past month; things as deep as sea tides in her, like looking at a perfectly calm stretch of tropic water, wanting to bathe in it and finding, just as the tide takes your body, that monsters dwell just under the surface, things unseen, bloated, many-armed, sharp-finned, malignant and inescapable.

A room floated around her in an effluvium of hysteria. Sharp instruments hovered and there were voices, and people in sterile white masks.

My name, she thought, what is it?

Alice Leiber. It came to her. David Leiber's wife. But it gave her no comfort. She was alone with these silent, whispering white people and there was great pain and nausea and death-fear in her.

I am being murdered before their eyes. These doctors, these nurses don't realize what hidden thing has happened to me. David doesn't know. Nobody knows except me and—the killer, the little murderer, the small assassin.

I am dying and I can't tell them now. They'd laugh and call me one in delirium. They'll see the murderer and hold him and never think him responsible for my death. But here I am, in front of God and man, dying, no one to believe my story, everyone to doubt me, comfort me with lies, bury me in ignorance, mourn me and salvage my destroyer.

Where is David? she wondered. In the waiting room, smoking one cigarette after another, listening to the long tickings of the very slow clock?

Sweat exploded from all of her body at once, and

with it an agonized cry. Now. Now! Try and kill me, she screamed. Try, try, but I won't die! I won't!

There was a hollowness. A vacuum. Suddenly the pain fell away. Exhaustion, and dusk came around. It was over. Oh, God! She plummeted down and struck a black nothingness which gave way to nothingness and nothingness and another and still another. . . .

Footsteps. Gentle, approaching footsteps.

Far away, a voice said, "She's asleep. Don't disturb her."

An odor of tweeds, a pipe, a certain shaving lotion. David was standing over her. And beyond him the immaculate smell of Dr. Jeffers.

She did not open her eyes. "I'm awake," she said, quietly. It was a surprise, a relief to be able to speak, to not be dead.

"Alice," someone said, and it was David beyond her closed eyes, holding her tired hands.

Would you like to meet the murderer, David? she thought. I hear your voice asking to see him, so there's nothing but for me to point him out to you.

David stood over her. She opened her eyes. The room came into focus. Moving a weak hand, she pulled aside a coverlet.

The murderer looked up at David Leiber with a small,

red-faced, blue-eyed calm. Its eyes were deep and sparkling.

"Why!" cried David Leiber, smiling. "He's a *fine* baby!"

Something Wicked This Way Comes

For those who still dream and remember, for those yet to experience the hypnotic power of its dark poetry, step inside. The show is about to begin. The carnival rolls in sometime after midnight, ushering in Halloween a week early. The shrill siren song of a calliope beckons to all with a seductive promise of dreams and youth regained. In this season of dying, Cooger & Dark's Pandemonium Shadow Show has come to Green Town, Illinois, to destroy every life touched by its strange and sinister mystery. And two boys will discover the secret of its smoke, mazes, and mirrors; two friends who will soon know all too well the heavy cost of wishes . . . and the stuff of nightmare.

Midnight then and the town clocks chiming on toward one and two and then three in the deep morning and the peals of the great clocks shaking dust off old toys in high attics and shedding silver off old mirrors in yet higher attics and stirring up dreams about clocks in all the beds where children slept.

Will heard it.

Muffled away in the prairie lands, the chuffing of an engine, the slow-following dragon-glide of a train.

Will sat up in bed.

Across the way, like a mirror image, Jim sat up, too.

A calliope began to play oh so softly, grieving to itself, a million miles away.

In one single motion, Will leaned from his window, as did Jim. Without a word they gazed over the trembling surf of trees.

Their rooms were high, as boys' rooms should be. From these gaunt windows they could rifle-fire their gaze artillery distances past library, city hall, depot, cow barns, farmlands to empty prairie!

There, on the world's rim, the lovely snail-gleam of the railway tracks ran, flinging wild gesticulations of lemon or cherry-colored semaphore to the stars.

There, on the precipice of earth, a small steam feather uprose like the first of a storm cloud yet to come.

The train itself appeared, link by link, engine, coal-car, and numerous and numbered all-asleep-and-slumbering-dreamfilled cars that followed the firefly-sparked churn, chant, drowsy autumn hearthfire roar. Hellfires flushed the stunned hills. Even at this remote view, one imagined men with buffalo-haunched arms shoveling black meteor falls of coal into the open boilers of the engine.

The engine!

Both boys vanished, came back to lift binoculars. "The engine!"

"Civil War! No other stack like that since 1900!"

"The rest of the train, *all* of it's old!"

"The flags! The cages! It's the carnival!"

They listened. At first Will thought he heard the air whistling fast in his nostrils. But no—it was the train, and the calliope sighing, weeping, on that train.

"Sounds like church music!"

"Hell. Why would a carnival play church music?"

"Don't say hell," hissed Will.

"Hell." Jim ferociously leaned out. "I've saved up all day. Everyone's asleep so—hell!"

The music drifted by their windows. Goose pimples rose big as boils on Will's arms.

"That *is* church music. Changed."

"For cri-yi, I'm froze, let's go watch them set up!"

"At three A.M.?"

"At three A.M.!"

Jim vanished.

For a moment, Will watched Jim dance around over there, shirt uplifted, pants going on, while off in night country, panting, churning was this funeral train all black plumed cars, licorice-colored cages, and a sooty calliope clamoring, banging three different hymns mixed and lost, maybe not there at all.

"Here goes nothing!"

Jim slid down the drainpipe on his house, toward the sleeping lawns.

"Jim! Wait!"

Will thrashed into his clothes.

"Jim, don't go *alone!*"

And followed after.

Death Is a Lonely Business

A fantastical tale of mayhem and murder set among the shadows and the murky canals of Venice, California, in the early 1950s. Toiling away amid the looming palm trees and decaying bungalows, a struggling young writer spins fantastic stories from his fertile imagination upon his clacking typewriter. The nameless writer steadily crafts his literary effort—until strange things begin happening around him. As the incidents escalate, his friends fall victim to a series of mysterious "accidents"—some of them fatal. Aided by a savvy, street-smart detective and a reclusive actress of yesteryear with an intense hunger for life, the wordsmith sets out to find the connection between the bizarre events, and in doing so, uncovers the truth about his own creative abilities.

Venice, California, in the old days had much to recommend it to people who liked to be sad. It had fog almost every night and along the shore the moaning of the oil well machinery and the slap of dark water in the canals and the hiss of sand against the windows of your house when the wind came up and sang among the open places and along the empty walks.

Those were the days when the Venice pier was falling apart and dying in the sea and you could find there the bones of a vast dinosaur, the rollercoaster, being covered by the shifting tides.

At the end of one long canal you could find old circus wagons that had been rolled and dumped, and in the cages, at midnight, if you looked, things lived—fish and crayfish moving with the tide; and it was all the circuses of time somehow gone to doom and rusting away.

And there was a loud avalanche of big red trolley car that rushed toward the sea every half-hour and at midnight skirled the curve and threw sparks on the high wires and rolled away with a moan which was like the dead turning in their sleep, as if the trolleys and the lonely men who swayed steering them knew that in another year they would be gone, the tracks covered with concrete and tar and the high spider-wire collected on rolls and spirited away.

And it was in that time, in one of those lonely years when the fogs never ended and the winds never stopped their laments, that riding the old red trolley, the highbucketing thunder, one night I met up with Death's friend and didn't know it.

It was a raining night, with me reading a book in the back of the old, whining, roaring railcar on its way from one empty confetti-tossed transfer station to the next. Just me and the big, aching wooden car and the conductor up front slamming the brass controls and easing the brakes and letting out the hell-steam when needed.

And the man down the aisle who somehow had got there without my noticing.

I became aware of him finally because of him swaying, swaying, standing there behind me for a long time, as if undecided because there were forty empty seats and late at night it is hard with so much emptiness to decide which one to take. But finally I heard him sit and I knew he was there because I could smell him like the tidelands coming in across the fields. On top of the smell of his clothes, there was the odor of too much drink taken in too little time.

I did not look back at him. I learned long ago, looking only encourages.

I shut my eyes and kept my head firmly turned away. It didn't work.

"Oh," the man moaned.

I could feel him strain forward in his seat. I felt his hot breath on my neck. I held on to my knees and sank away.

"Oh," he moaned, even louder. It was like someone falling off a cliff, asking to be saved, or someone swimming far out in the storm, wanting to be seen.

"Ah!"

It was raining hard now as the big red trolley bucketed across a midnight stretch of meadow-grass and the rain banged the windows, drenching away the sight of open fields. We sailed through Culver City without seeing the film studio and ran on, the great car heaving, the floorboard whining underfoot, the empty seats creaking, the train whistle screaming.

And a blast of terrible air from behind me as the unseen man cried, "Death!"

The train whistle cut across his voice so he had to start over.

"Death—"

Another whistle.

"Death," said the voice behind me, "is a lonely business."

A Graveyard for Lunatics

Halloween night, 1954. A young, film-obsessed scriptwriter has just been hired at one of the great studios. An anonymous invitation leads him from the giant Maximus Films backlot to an eerie graveyard separated from the studio by a single wall. There he makes a terrifying discovery that thrusts him into a maelstrom of intrigue and mystery—and into the dizzy exhilaration of the movie industry at the height of its glittering power.

Once upon a time there were two cities within a city. One was light and one was dark. One moved restlessly all day while the other never stirred. One was warm and filled with ever-changing lights. One was cold and fixed in place by stones. And when the sun went down each afternoon on Maximus Films, the city of the living, it began to resemble Green Glades cemetery just across the way, which was the city of the dead.

As the lights went out and the motions stopped and the wind that blew around the corners of the studio buildings cooled, an incredible melancholy seemed to sweep from the front gate of the living all the way along through twilight avenues toward that high brick wall that separated the two cities within a city. And suddenly the streets were filled with something one could speak of only as remembrance. For while the people had gone away, they left behind them architectures that were haunted by the ghosts of incredible happenings.

For indeed it was the most outrageous city in the world, where anything could happen and always did. Ten thousand deaths had happened here, and when the deaths were done, the people got up, laughing, and strolled away. Whole tenement blocks were set afire and did not burn. Sirens shrieked and police cars careened around corners, only to have the officers peel off their blues, cold-cream their orange pancake makeup, and walk home to small bungalow court apartments out in that great and mostly boring world.

Dinosaurs prowled here, one moment in miniature, and the next looming fifty feet tall above half-clad virgins who screamed on key. From here various Crusades departed to peg their armor and stash their spears at Western Costume down the road. From here Henry the Eighth let drop some heads. From here Dracula wandered as flesh to return as dust. Here also were the Stations of the Cross and a trail of ever-replenished blood as screenwriters groaned by to Calvary carrying a back-breaking load of revisions, pursued by directors with scourges and film cutters with razor-sharp knives. It was from these towers that the Muslim faithful were called to worship each day at sunset as the limousines whispered out with faceless powers behind each window, and peasants averted their gaze, fearing to be struck blind.

This being true, all the more reason to believe that when the sun vanished the old haunts rose up, so that the warm city cooled and began to resemble the marbled orchardways across the wall. By midnight, in that strange peace caused by temperature and wind and the voice of some far church clock, the two cities were at last one. And the night watchman was the only motion prowling along from India to France to prairie Kansas to brownstone New York to Piccadilly to the Spanish Steps, covering twenty thousand miles of territorial incredibility in twenty brief minutes. Even as his counterpart across the wall punched the time clocks around among the monuments, flashed his light on various Arctic angels, read names like credits on tombstones, and sat to have his midnight tea with all that was left of some Keystone Kop. At four in the morning, the watchmen asleep, the two cities, folded and kept, waited for the sun to rise over withered flowers, eroded tombs, and elephant India ripe for overpopulation should God the Director decree and Central Casting deliver.

And so it was on All Hallows Eve, 1954.

Halloween.

My favorite night in all the year.